DiVA

It's a GiRL ThiNG

DIVA

It's a GIRL Thing

Sue Lawson

BACKPACKBOOKS

NEW YORK

This 2007 edition published by Backpack Books
by arrangement with

black dog books,
15 Gertrude Street, Fitzroy, Victoria 3065, Australia.

Designed by Blue Boat Design

ISBN-13: 978-0-7607-9670-2
ISBN-10: 0-7607-9670-X

Printed and bound by Everbest Printing Co Ltd, China

1 3 5 7 9 10 8 6 4 2

Contents

Book One
It's a Girl Thing 1

Book Two
Going Solo 59

Book Three
Finale 125

Glossary 192

Quizzes 194

Quiz Answers 200

Sensational singer?
Dynamic dancer?
Cool, calm, confident?
Be our Dream Diva!

Girls Stuff magazine and
Dream Productions are looking for
the nation's best young female talent.
So if you're a sensational singer,
dynamic dancer and under 16,
get Mom or Dad's okay, fill out the entry
form and rock up to our national auditions.
Go for it, Dream Diva!

Contents

Chapter One 5

Chapter Two 12

Chapter Three 19

Chapter Four 25

Chapter Five 30

Chapter Six 35

Chapter Seven 38

Chapter Eight 46

Chapter Nine 49

Chapter One

I'm Mickey Farrell, the youngest girl in a family of three. My sisters, Sam and Gemma, are sports-tragics. You name it and they not only play it, but they win every trophy possible.

They dream of being sporting legends.

I dream of being a singing star.

A month ago I was lying on my bed reading *Girls Stuff*, when the Dream Productions advertisement practically jumped off the page. Imagine — the hottest CDs, cool clothes and heaps of fans. It would be a dream come true!

I'd filled out the entry form, talked

Mom into signing it and then posted it, all before my sisters had finished watching the Tropicana Triathlon.

Yep, a month ago that ad was the pathway to my dreams.

But today, sitting here in this massive university hall filled with a thousand other girls, I'm not so sure.

My hands are shaking.

My knees feel like rubber.

And a billion butterflies have invaded my stomach.

This is crazy. I've sung at talent quests, sung and danced in concerts and I've been in musical productions. But not once did I feel like this.

Maybe I wouldn't feel so bad if my friends Charley and Hana were with me. Yeah right! As if they'd be here. Hana would rather be scrapbooking and you couldn't part Charley from her horse, even if there was a national emergency.

I smooth my new three-quarter jeans and brush a speck of fluff off my Express T-shirt.

I look around, trying to distract myself from the butterflies in my stomach and my rubber knees. Mom's beside me, tapping away at her laptop finishing some report due Monday, like nothing major is happening. The girl to my left is reading. She twirls her hair around her finger, uncurls it and twirls it again.

Behind me, a kid with her hair parted on the side and pulled back into a sleek ponytail chews gum. She's watching the four girls leaning together, heads almost touching. They look around and giggle behind their hands. A shudder runs down my spine. Girls like that freak me out.

What's freaking me out even more is the woman with the crow-black bob scanning the crowd with narrowed

eyes. Her fingers tap against her folded arms. The jewels in her flashy rings splash tiny rainbows on the wall. Beside her, her daughter sighs and examines her fingernails. I can tell it's the freaky woman's daughter because they both have the same snooty noses and crow-black hair.

Feedback squeals through the speakers.

A blond guy wearing jeans and a surf T-shirt steps up to the microphone. "Welcome to the Dream Diva state auditions. I'm your host, Jed Somerton."

Polite applause fills the room.

"So you guys want to be stars, right?"

People mumble and shift in their seats.

"Singing stars with recording contracts and film clips."

Parents clap. Girls whistle and squeal "Yeah!"

"You want to be the Dream Diva."

Everyone goes off!

Jed grins and points his fingers, pistol-like. "Well, let's get to it."

"He's kind of cute," says Mom, finally lifting her eyes from her laptop.

I sigh and push my hand against my tummy. Stupid butterflies.

"Here's the deal — you guys audition today and another thousand girls face the judges tomorrow." He paces the stage, nodding. "Only eight girls will go through to round two. We'll find out who they are tomorrow afternoon."

My stomach flipped like a performing dolphin. Two thousand of us competing for eight places. This was going to be hard work!

Jed winks and clicks his fingers. "Remember, we'll be filming for the Dream Diva TV series, so big smiles, everyone!" He does this bizarre smile

and points to his perfect teeth. "Righto, Divas, let's go. There are posters all around the room, printed with numbers in blocks of ten. Check out the number on your wristband and find that number on the poster."

What's he talking about? I poke the pink band on my wrist. The number 351 is printed between two silver stars. I can see the huge pink numbers "350-360" on a poster to my right. A tall girl with butter-colored hair, wearing a pink Dream Diva T-shirt, stands under the poster.

Jed is talking again. "Your gorgeous supervisor is waiting for you. She'll take care of you till your parents return later today." Fingers click, there's a wink, then Jed slaps an open hand against his wrist. If I wasn't feeling so churned up, I'd giggle.

"Okay, time to farewell the olds."

A pistol point to the main door. "Because, it's time to rock!"

The hooting, cheering and stamping of feet is deafening.

Mom closes her laptop and eases it into the leather case. "Well, Mickey, this is it." She leans forward and squeezes my arm. "The first step towards your dream."

If I say anything a million butterflies will pour out of my mouth.

"Dad and I are very proud of you, Mickey." Her eyes look glassy as she folds me into one of her bear hugs. She kisses my forehead. Once. Twice. Three times!

I wiggle out of her grip. "Mom! Go, already!"

"Love you, Mickey Moose."

I cringe at the sound of my family's nickname. "I love you, too."

Mom kisses me again, hitches her bag onto her shoulder and finally heads for the door.

Chapter Two

"Hi," says the supervisor with butter-colored hair. "I'm Zoë."

"I'm Mickey," I say, shaking her hand. She's wearing the best bead bracelet.

Within a minute, there are ten of us surrounding Zoë. The girl with the sleek ponytail is in my group and so is the girl with the freaky mom. There's no sign of the four whispering and giggling girls, thank goodness.

Zoë hands each of us a Dream Diva name tag. The girl with the sleek ponytail is Erin and the Mini-Freak is Coco.

"Grab a seat," says Zoë. "We'll start by introducing ourselves."

In her rush to sit next to Zoë, Coco jabs Erin in the stomach with her chair leg.

Erin glares at Coco, but says nothing.

"Who'd like to go first?" asks Zoë.

Why am I not surprised when Coco's hand shoots into the air?

"My name is Coco Lamont. I live in a two-story home overlooking Starlight Bay and attend Bennington Grammar. I play piano and cello. My little sister Bella and I are members of the Starlight Bay Musical Theatre Company. We've been going to Junior Starz Singing and Dancing School since we were three. And I've been lead in the Starz end-of-year production for three years, now. My style is classic pop with a dash of rock and rap."

She has so practiced that in front of the mirror.

"Thanks, Coco," says Zoë, turning to Erin.

"But I'm not finished," says Coco.

"I'm sure we'll hear more about you during the day." Zoë writes in her folder. "So, Erin, where are you from?"

Erin reminds me of Hana. She has similar hair and is wearing the same sort of stuff Hana loves — surf T-shirt and denim skirt.

"I live in Wilton with my mom and my brother, Jason. He's 14. My dad died when I was four." Erin shifts in her seat. "My mom enrolled me in dancing lessons a couple of years ago because she said I needed more exercise. I started singing lessons last year and I've done a couple of school plays, too. I represent my school in the regional talent quest every year. Is that enough?" Erin frowns at Zoë.

"Perfect, thanks Erin."

Mia and Demi go next, telling their stories a line at a time. They live at the beach, near the border, and go to the same school. Demi looks like a rock chick and wears a black bracelet that reminds me of a dog's collar. Mia's long hair is braided and tied with a rainbow ribbon.

Prani speaks three languages and can play the harp. Tessa sings in a church choir and plays touch football. Maddy writes her own songs and hates cats. Lisa is horse mad and Laura has played Little Cosette in a city production of *Les Miserables*.

"Lucky last, Mickey."

"I'm Mickey Farrell. I love singing and dancing, piano and music. Mom and Dad got sick of sitting through my made-up concerts, so they enrolled me in Lizzie Denton's Singing and Dance School. I think I was about three. Mom and Dad own an advertising company and my big sisters, Gemma and Sam, are sports mad. That's it, I guess."

"Is Lizzie your teacher, Mickey?" asks Zoë.

"Yeah, but she has other teachers working for her, too. Why?"

"I've known Lizzie for years. She's a top operator." Zoë smiles. "Okay, guys, you'll spend the morning rehearsing with me and at some stage this morning everyone will be interviewed by Jed for the TV show. You'll sing for the judges this afternoon."

"Who are the judges, Zoë?" asks Coco.

"Dream Productions manager Gwen Davies, *Misty Beach* star Sunshine Harris—"

"Cool!" I blurt out. I can't help it. Sunshine sings, dances and acts. Hana, Charley and I think she's the best!

"Go on, Zoë," says Coco, shooting me a weird look.

"And Johnny Mawton."

Johnny Mawton is on TV every night.

He hosts a current affair program and TV specials. Mom says he's over-exposed. I just reckon he's annoying.

"I read a rumour in *Weekly TV* that Johnny was a judge," says Coco, grinning like she knows something we don't.

"So, have you guys decided what you're singing for the judges?" asks Zoë.

A week after I posted my entry, a pink Dream Diva envelope had arrived, stuffed full of forms. Among the rules and papers to sign was a list of the five songs to choose from. *Somewhere Over the Rainbow* from *The Wizard of Oz*, *Locomotion*, *My Boy Lollipop*, *Celebrate* and *Dancing Queen*.

Tough choice. I mean, *Dancing Queen* is fun and *Celebrate* is cool, but seeing as I won last year's regional talent quest singing *Locomotion*, I figured I should sing that. At least that way I didn't have to learn anything new. It was a dangerous

choice though. Sports-Tragic Two, Gemma, threatened to slam dunk me if she heard *Locomotion* again, so I had to practice when she was out doing sport stuff.

Some of the others are doing *Dancing Queen*. Erin's singing *Celebrate*.

"I'm singing *My Boy Lollipop*," says Coco, fiddling with a loose thread on her halter-neck dress. "Pity there's no Madonna. I so sing like her."

Zoë raises her eyebrows and checks her watch. "Why don't we go to the rehearsal room, girls?"

Chapter Three

Zoë leads us out of the main hall and down a corridor.

"There are rehearsal rooms set up for today around the university," says Zoë, opening the third door with a Dream Diva logo on it.

Inside, mirrors line one wall. Bottles of water and soft drink, bowls of candy and baskets of fruit cover a long trestle along the opposite wall. A piano stands in the middle of the room.

"Unreal," says Erin.

"Zoë, why is there a piano here?" asks Lisa. "I thought we had to sing without music."

"You will sing without music for the judges. The piano's here so you can work with me. Hopefully I'll be able to give you a few tips." Zoë winks. "The rest of the time you can work on your own."

"Where are the cameras, Zoë?" asks Coco.

"You'll see them at lunch, when you perform for the judges and when Jed interviews you. And, of course, at tomorrow's announcement. But there are no cameras in the rehearsal room, at least not until round three." Zoë pulls a bundle of papers from her bag. "Trust me; if you go that far, the cameras will drive you nuts."

"Oh, I'll get there," says Coco, talking to the mirror.

"Then it won't be the cameras driving us nuts," whispers Erin.

I giggle.

Coco flashes me a deadly look.

I grab a handful of jelly beans and shove them in my mouth.

Coco stands facing the mirrors and sings scales.

"Is someone strangling a cat?" hisses Erin.

"Prani, you can work with me first," says Zoë.

Prani walks to the piano, face twisted, hands flapping. Everyone except Coco gathers around the piano to listen to Prani sing *Dancing Queen*. Her voice is strong and clear until she goes for the high notes. Erin notices Prani becoming frustrated, and gets us to sing along. Maddy and Demi dance and sing back-up.

By the end of the song, we're all laughing, even Zoë.

Once Prani is more relaxed, we wander off to do our own thing. Erin, Laura and I take it in turns singing.

Erin's voice is awesome. Strong and deep. Laura's is higher, sweeter. Erin and I encourage Laura to relax. Laura and Erin tell me the same thing my singing teacher Lizzie tells me. "Stand straight, shoulders back!"

We sing, eat jelly beans, chat, sing some more, encourage each other and eat more jelly beans.

After an hour, Zoë calls me to the piano. "Okay, Mickey, sing it straight through first."

Before I can ask her how she knows Lizzie, Zoë's counting me in.

Have you ever tried to sing with nine other people singing different songs in the same room? It's tough! After the first couple of lines I close my eyes and block out everything except the piano.

"Well done, Mickey. You're a talented girl."

Warmth floods my body.

We practice together for 20 minutes. Zoë is so cool and knows so much! She points out that I sometimes run words together and don't finish words cleanly. "Just relax in front of the judges, Mickey. You'll be great," says Zoë, patting my arm.

As she calls Coco, I head back over to where Laura and Erin are sitting cross-legged on the floor, a bowl of candy between them. Prani and Lisa join us.

"How cool is Zoë?" I say, taking a handful of candy.

"She's the best," says Lisa.

"I don't know about Coco, though," says Prani. "She's kind of freaky."

"You think she's freaky. You should see her mother," I say. "Coco's just the Mini-Freak."

We burst out laughing.

"She's a seriously good singer though," I say.

"Don't be so nice," says Erin, throwing a red snake at me.

"I reckon Mickey, Erin and Coco will make it through easy," says Laura.

My face flushes. "Coco and Erin will, but—"

"Serious, Mickey. You're great!"

The alarm on Zoë's mobile phone sounds. She bundles her papers and slips them back into her bag. "Righto, girls, grab your gear."

"What now, Zoë?" asks Mini-Freak.

"Interviews!"

Chapter Four

Zoë stops outside a green door with "The Green Room" printed on a brass plaque.

"Well, duh," says Erin, nodding at the sign. "As if we need a sign to tell us it's green!"

Coco rolls her eyes and puts a hand on her hip. "Honestly, Erin. You are so rural. The Green Room is where singers wait before going on stage."

Erin stares at her feet. Her face is bright pink.

My skin prickles.

"Not everyone has heard of the Green Room, Coco." Zoë flips open her folder briskly. "Jed will interview you in small

groups. The rest of us will wait in the dressing room." Zoë looks at her folder. "Erin, Coco and...'

I hold my breath. It'd be cool to be interviewed with Erin, but with Coco? No way.

"...Mickey. You're first, girls." She opens the door and ushers us inside.

Old concert posters cover the green walls. A black chair faces a pink couch.

Two cameras face the couch. A third is strapped to a camera operator.

I wipe my palms on my legs. "This is freaky."

"I reckon," whispers Erin.

Coco snorts and flounces towards the couch.

I nudge Erin forward and sit between them.

"Good morning, Divas," says Jed, bouncing into the room. "Having fun?"

Erin and I nod.

"Definitely," says Coco, checking her reflection in the small mirror she's pulled from her bag.

Sound guys attach microphones to our tops. Make-up girls powder our faces.

"Any questions?" asks Jed.

Erin and I shake our heads. Coco opens her mouth, but Jed cuts her off before she can speak. "Then, let's rock."

The Interview...

Jed: *So guys, how's your day been?*

Erin: *Cool.*

Mickey: *Great fun. We've been hanging out in the rehearsal room, helping each other practice.*

Coco: *It's great to spend time with such talented girls. I'm learning so much from them.*

Jed: *Okay...So, what do your school friends think of you trying out today?*

 **DIVA**

Coco: *My school, Bennington Grammar, is incredibly supportive of talent. Everyone just knows I'll do well.*

Jed: *What about your friends, Mickey?*

Mickey: *I haven't told them, and I've sworn Mom, Dad and my sisters to secrecy.*

Jed: *How come?*

Mickey: *In case I don't make it past the auditions.*

Coco: *Wise move.*

Erin: *Gosh, Mickey, I've told anyone who'll listen. Most people are mega-excited for me. My nan sent me this cute ballerina bear and a huge bunch of flowers.*

Jed: *Erin, why did you enter Dream Diva?*

Erin: *(Shrugs.) I love singing and dancing and I guess Dream Diva sounded like fun.*

Coco: *Yes, fun. And a great opportunity to fast-track my career. Although, I'm already acknowledged as being well on my way.*

Mickey: *Erin has an amazing voice. And she has a real presence when she sings.*

Coco: *She moves quite well, considering she's never had a dancing lesson.*

Erin: *I have…in Wilton.*

Coco: *That's hardly a real lesson is it?*

Jed: *Mickey. What do you hope to get out of the audition process?*

Mickey: *Well, I've made a new friend, so anything above that is a bonus.*

Coco: *Which is good, seeing as you've never performed in anything major.*

Jed: *How are you feeling about facing the judges, girls?*

Erin: *A bit nervous.*

Mickey: *Yeah, like they're huge. Gwen knows talent, Sunshine's so good, and Johnny Mawton's — well he's scary.*

Coco: *When you have the experience I do, facing the judges isn't a problem. I mean—*

Jed: *Gosh, Divas, we're out of time. Good luck today, but most of all have fun.*

Coco: *Any tips, Jed?*

Jed: *Yeah, Coco. Just sing.*

Chapter Five

Zoë and the rest of our group rush towards us as we enter the dressing room.

"So, how'd it go?"

"What did Jed ask?"

"Is he cute up-close?"

Coco the Mini-Freak tosses her head. "It was a breeze."

"Prani, Maddy, Tessa and Lisa, you're next," says Zoë consulting her folder.

As they head to the Green Room, I call over my shoulder. "Good luck, guys."

Erin and I make for the back corner.

"I was hopeless," says Erin, fishing a furry jelly baby from her jeans pocket.

"No you weren't!"

She rolls her eyes.

"How about Mini-Freak? She's so confident."

"I'm not sure that's good. I mean she can sing, but..." I say.

"I watch the way Coco moves her hands and tosses her hair. She reminds me of a movie star."

"...she bugs me."

"Me too," says Erin, still picking fluff from her jelly bean. "And her clothes. That dress would look better on Zoë."

For the next 40 minutes, while Jed interviews the rest of the group, we hang out in the dressing room talking to Zoë about performing, using microphones and stage fright. It'd be better if Coco would shut up!

"My dance teacher says..."

"When I hold a microphone..."

"Can't say I've ever had stage fright..."

Blah, blah, blah. I try to block out her voice and concentrate on Zoë's hints.

When Mia, Laura and Demi return, Zoë checks her watch. "Time for lunch."

Instead of a sea of chairs, the main hall is now filled with trestle tables. Each table has a white tablecloth with tiny pink and silver stars scattered over it. Silver string anchors bundles of hot-pink helium balloons to huge pewter stars. Two bright pink buckets filled with ice hold bottles of soft drink — cola, orange and lemonade.

It looks great but the food smells even better. Foccacias. Gourmet pizzas. Pies. Hot dogs. Hamburgers. Chicken...hot, cold or fried. Chips. Even salads!

And for dessert — mud cakes, fruit salad, sundaes, caramel slices, cheesecakes, donuts, yogurt and every flavour of ice cream you can imagine. My stomach rumbles.

"Choose whatever you like and grab a table," says Zoë, fishing her beeping phone out of her bag. She reads the screen and grins. "We face the judges around 2:30."

The moment Zoë mentions the judges, those stupid butterflies are back, fluttering like crazy

Zoë slips her phone back into her bag. "I'll be back soon."

Erin and I stroll to the serving area.

"Pig out!" she says, passing me a plate.

"Nah. My stomach's churning. Think I'll stick to something light."

I grab a chicken, cheese and avocado foccacia and chips. Followed by a caramel sundae. And an orange soft drink.

"So that's a light lunch," says Coco, across the table.

"Are you feeding your pet rabbit, Coco?" asks Erin, nodding at the lettuce, carrot and sprouts piled on Coco's plate. It looks like some ad from a health magazine.

Coco sneers.

 **DIVA**

I lift my drink to my mouth, hoping it covers my smile. While we're eating, Mia and Demi tell us hilarious stories about their school teacher.

"We call him Harry Highpants," says Demi, hitching up her jeans.

"And he wears a ginger wig. Really! You can tell it's a wig because the hair around his ears is black."

Lisa laughs so hard, cola comes out her nose. My sides ache from laughing.

"Honestly," says Coco, folding her napkin.

She places her cutlery together on her plate as if she's finished. It looks like she's just moved her food around a bit rather than eaten anything. She's shaking her head like a disapproving parent.

"Looks like you're having fun," says Zoë, walking up to the table. "Ready for a last practice?"

That stops our laughter!

Chapter Six

The spring sunshine warms my back as I follow Zoë along a path lined with trees. She leads us through double glass-doors. "This is your last chance to rehearse before you face the judges."

"Zoë, can I sing for the judges while the others rehearse?" asks Coco.

"We audition together, Coco."

"You mean we perform in front of the judges and each other?" asks Prani, her face white.

"So you'll be able to support each other. Come on, time's wasting. Let's get to work," says Zoë.

This time, the mood while we practice

is different. Everyone works alone. Zoë moves around, encouraging us.

I start with the warm-ups my singing teacher, Lizzie, taught me — face stretches, raspberries and singing as high and low as I can. I shake my arms and legs to loosen my muscles. I sing *Locomotion* trying to remember everything Lizzie and Zoë have taught me.

"Ten minutes, guys," calls Zoë.

I sit on the ground, legs crossed and eyes closed, doing the visualization stuff my sisters, the Sports-Tragics, swear by. Before every game, they imagine themselves playing well. Before last year's talent quest, I tried it out. I imagined myself singing perfectly. When I stepped onto the stage, I did the best performance ever. I'm not convinced it works, but it does settle the butterflies and my wobbly knees.

"Are you feeling okay?"

I open my eyes. Erin is standing over me, frowning. "Yeah. Just running through my song."

Erin squats and whispers, "Check out Mini-Freak."

Across the room, Coco is rubbing stuff onto her cheeks. There's a can of hair spray, a brush and comb, tubs of make-up and a mirror all lined up on the floor in front of her.

"I didn't even bring a brush," I say.

Erin hands me hers. "Do you want to borrow my lip-gloss too?"

"Nah, I always have one," I say, pulling it from my pocket.

Zoë clears her throat. "This is it, guys. Time to go."

The color drains from Erin's face.

"You'll be fantastic, I know it!" I say.

"Thanks, Mickey. You don't need luck," she says.

"I wish!"

Chapter Seven

The judges' room isn't a hall, like I expected. It's only as big as my classroom except, unlike my classroom, everything is pink and silver. Pink helium balloons cover the ceiling. The silver stage and backdrop are printed with the Dream Diva logo. Three pink office-chairs are behind a desk with the Dream Diva logo, and a row of pink chairs line the stage.

"Grab a seat. Gwen, Sunshine and Johnny are on their way here," says Zoë, smiling.

The air presses on my skin, thick and heavy. Everyone, even Coco, looks totally freaked out. It takes all my courage not to sprint out the door.

One of the balloons drops a little until the string is within my reach. I pull it towards me. With my back turned to the rest of my group, I unclip the balloon and suck in a big breath of helium.

I take my seat beside Erin, balloon on my lap. "I think I have a jelly baby stuck in my throat." I sound like Donald Duck. "Will the judges notice?"

Everyone, even Zoë, bursts out laughing. Coco rolls her eyes. The thick, heavy feeling lifts.

"What?" I say, faking surprise, my voice still very Donald Duck-ish. "What's so funny?"

The laughter's so loud we don't hear the judges enter.

"You're a relaxed group." The voice is warm and rich. Gwen Davies, Dream Productions' manager, sits in the middle chair.

"My dad sucked in helium once.

I thought I'd die laughing," says Sunshine Harris, smiling at me.

"Very dangerous. We did a report on *Behind the Headlines* about the hazards of breathing in helium." Johnny Mawton flips his tie and adjusts his suit jacket.

I release the balloon. It zips around the room, smashing against the windows and backdrop before landing in a crumpled heap on the judges' desk. Everyone laughs except Johnny who just shakes his head.

Zoë walks over to the table and talks to the judges. Sunshine gives me a wink. My stomach flutters. Sunshine Harris, one of my heroes, winking at me! Wait till I tell Hana and Charley!

Zoë hands Johnny a sheet of paper. "Girls, when Johnny calls your name, step up to the stage and sing until you're asked to stop. And...," Zoë claps her hands and smiles, "...have fun!"

"It's been a long, hard morning, ladies.

Here's hoping we see a little more talent than some of the groups we've seen." Johnny's mouth smiles, but his eyes stay hard. "Any questions?"

The others shake their heads.

I say "no" mainly because I want to make sure all the helium has left my throat! Which it has.

"Okay, 359. Prani, you're first."

We all clap and hoot.

"Go Prani!" I call.

Hardly daring to breathe, I watch Prani, then Maddy, Tessa and Lisa perform. They sing for barely 40 seconds before Johnny raises his hand to stop them. The judges' whispers and note-taking takes longer than each performance.

Laura's left leg shakes so much she slips off the stage. The judges don't ask her to start again. Both Mia and Demi try to keep singing after Johnny stops

them. That only makes his neck turn red. My knees are jigging up and down by the time Johnny calls Erin's name.

"Go for it." I squeeze her hand.

She smiles then, head high, steps onto the stage.

"I'm singing *Celebrate*," she says.

Her voice is shaky. I bite my lip. Johnny lifts his arm. Sunshine stops him.

Erin's voice settles. She sounds confident and strong. A huge grin spreads across my face.

"Well done, Erin," says Johnny.

Erin beams. She's sung for longer than anyone else so far.

Johnny checks his piece of paper. "Umm, 351, Mickey Farrell."

I hope my rubbery knees will hold me up.

"Good work, Erin," I whisper as we pass.

She grins. "Go for it, Mickey!"

The words to *Locomotion* fill my head as I step onto the stage. I clench and unclench my fists.

"Has the helium cleared?" asks Sunshine, grinning.

"Hope so!"

"So do we," says Johnny.

My jelly knees wobble. I take a deep breath and sing. The first line flows. By the second, my knees feel stronger. I make eye contact with Gwen, then Sunshine. I finish the third verse.

"Enough thanks, Nicky."

My stomach plummets to my toes. Johnny hasn't even got my name right.

"Mickey," Sunshine corrects him. "Great effort."

My smile feels weak. I step off the stage, barely registering my group's cheers.

"Lucky last, Coco Lamont," says Johnny.

Coco breezes past me, smiling sweetly. "You sound better full of helium," she mutters.

I slump in my seat and stare at the purple shoes Mom bought me especially for today.

"You were fantastic, Mickey," says Erin.

"I was rubbish," I mutter.

"Isn't the expression, save the best till last?" says Coco to the judges.

I so want to vomit. On her!

"Sunshine, Gwen, Johnny. I'm Coco Lamont and I'm an experienced—"

"Just sing," says Johnny sharply.

"Of course." Coco clears her voice and launches into *Somewhere over the Rainbow*, which is pretty surprising seeing as she's practiced *My Boy Lollipop* all day.

I watch the second hand on my watch — 10, 20, 30, 45 seconds, 60 seconds.

As much as I hate to admit it, Coco is good. Johnny's eyes are glassy and he's swaying. Great!

"Okay, thanks, Coco," says Sunshine, elbowing Johnny.

"Magnificent, Coco." Johnny's voice is soft.

"Oh please," hisses Erin.

Zoë steps onto the stage. "That's it guys. Have a bite to eat back in the main hall before your parents pick you up."

"We'll see you back here tomorrow at 3:00 p.m. for our verdict," says Johnny.

I feel like all the air has been sucked out of me. Before following Mia and Demi to the door, I turn back to the judges. "Thanks for listening." I muster a big smile.

Sunshine and Gwen beam back.

"Pleasure!"

"Thanks, Mickey."

Johnny doesn't look up from his notes.

Chapter Eight

Back in the main hall, groups of girls sit at tables eating blueberry, chocolate, and orange muffins. A few are drinking hot chocolates, but most are slurping milkshakes.

"Let's hang out together till our parents come," says Prani, heading for the people making milkshakes.

I order a Mars Bar milkshake and a blueberry muffin. We gather at a table by the main door.

"What's the deal with her doing *Over the Rainbow*?" asks Erin, slipping into the seat beside me.

"The deal is," says Coco, behind us,

"unlike you amateurs, I do my research. When I read the rumour in Weekly TV that Johnny Mawton was a judge, I checked out his website. Guess what his favorite song is? *Somewhere over the Rainbow*." She pats my shoulder. "Looks like I'm through to round two." She struts to a seat by the officials' table.

"She is so, so..." The words won't come.

"She'll get hers," says Erin.

We've barely started our milkshakes and muffins, when parents begin wandering through the doors.

While we chat about the judging, I see Mini-Freak's mom.

"That haircut sure stands out," says Erin.

Mrs. Freak makes a beeline for Coco. Coco slings her bag over her shoulder and waves at us with three fingers while her mom signs her out.

"Hey, there's my mom." Erin whistles. Her mom spins around and smiles. She's fairer than Erin, but her eyes have the same twinkle.

I spot Mom near the stage and wave. She charges in my direction. The crowd parts for her. She has that effect, especially when she's wearing her black suit.

"Mickey Moose." She wraps me in one of her hugs. "How did it go?"

"She was great," says Erin.

Our moms chat for a bit, while Erin and I plan to meet inside the main doors at 2:50 p.m. tomorrow.

Chapter Nine

What a night! Mom and Dad grill me with a thousand and one questions.

Was it fun?

What was Johnny like?

Is Sunshine really tiny?

How did I sing?

What was the food like?

Lucky for me, the Sports-Tragics are at a basketball camp this weekend, so I don't have to put up with their questions, too.

I feel more tired than I can ever remember so I go to bed straight after dinner and sleep till late the next morning. Even so, the day is dragging.

I watch cartoons and music videos for

ages and tidy my room — not that I'm a neat freak, I'm just desperate to keep my mind off the whole Diva thing.

After what feels like days, but is really only hours, Mom and I are standing inside the hall, waiting for Erin.

The hall's set up the same way it was when we arrived yesterday. Only today there are more people. The noise is amazing. A rumble of voices, scraping chairs and music.

I scan the crowd for Erin. Coco and her mother are easier to find. I watch their black heads glide to the front of the hall. They remind me of a knife cutting a cake.

Coco's wearing a sequined top with a full skirt. Seriously "look at me" clothes. Suddenly my monkey-cartoon T-shirt and my green skirt feel more "kinder-kid" than the "smart-casual" I was going for.

"Those two are definitely freaky." Erin stands beside me, grinning.

"Definitely," I say.

A voice booms over the intercom. "Ladies and gentlemen please be seated. The judges are on their way."

"Let's sit near the front," says Erin, rushing forward. She plunks her butt in a seat five rows from the stage. Our moms follow.

The lights dip, silencing the crowd. A dance track thumps out of the speakers. A spotlight hits the stage.

Jed bops towards the microphone. I hadn't noticed it earlier, but Gwen, Sunshine and Johnny's judging table is set up in the middle of the stage.

"Welcome to the Dream Diva judges' decision!"

The hall erupts in hoots and whistles.

He points and clicks like crazy. "Okay, so who's going on to round two?"

The crowd goes seriously off.

The butterflies in my stomach are

 **DIVA**

replaced by stampeding cattle. How can the judges choose eight girls from 2,000?

Erin grabs my hand. "No matter what, let's stay friends. We'll email and stuff."

"For sure!" My throat feels tight.

Jed talks a little about the judges' backgrounds and the whole Diva competition, but I can't concentrate. I keep re-living yesterday's performance, thinking of all the things I did wrong.

Sucking in helium.

Singing too quickly.

Running my words together.

Applause and wolf whistles snap me back to reality.

The judges settle into their pink chairs behind the desk. Sunshine and Gwen smile and wave. Johnny nods. I look around for Zoë. She's standing to the left of the stage with the other supervisors. I wonder if she knows who's made it.

"So guys, how was the talent?" asks Jed.

"Amazing," says Gwen.

"I wish we didn't have to choose," says Sunshine.

"But we do, and it's my job to announce the names of the eight winners of this state's auditions." Johnny flips his tie and consults a piece of paper.

Before he can continue, Gwen leans toward the microphone. "Girls, you're all to be congratulated on your efforts this weekend. Auditions are hard work and you handled yourselves well. We watched two thousand terrific performances."

"Exactly. As I call your name, ladies, join us on stage. The first of the eight girls going through is…" Johnny lists numbers and names as though he is calling the lotto draw. I try to concentrate but my brain is mush.

"Contestant 357, Erin Chang."

Erin leaps to her feet, squealing.

My mom and Mrs. Chang hug her.

I jump up and hug her too.

"You're next!" She squeezes my hand and jogs toward the stage.

"Number 358, Coco Lamont."

"Number 696, Bree Swann."

In the front row, Freak is smoothing Mini-Freak's eyebrows. Mini-Freak tosses her raven hair and struts towards the stage.

"Number 795, Ginny Di Santo."

The butterflies in my stomach die. My shoulders droop. I've missed out.

My mom squeezes my knee. I can't look at her.

"Number 1,006, Miffy Carr."

"Number 1,231, Saraid McTaggert."

I scrunch down low and pick up Mom's bag. "We may as well go."

"Number 1,835, Margie Ng."

"And, the last person through to the next round of Dream Diva..."

"Beat the crowd," I mutter.

Mom screams like I've just bitten her. She shakes my arm, still squealing. Now Mrs. Chang joins in.

"Please," I hiss. "I'm feeling bad enough. Do you have to make a spectacle of me?"

"Mickey! Mickey!" says Mom.

Maybe she's having a stroke.

Then I hear it "Repeating, 351 — Mickey Farrell. Where are you, Mickey?"

Mrs. Chang leaps to her feet and points at me. "She's here!"

I slowly straighten up. Mom shoves me in the middle of the back. I stumble forward.

Zoë waves me towards the stage. Erin jumps up and down, clapping.

"We kept Mickey till last for a reason," says Gwen, taking over from Johnny.

Great! Now she's going to say I'm a dud, but the judges felt sorry for me.

"Over the past two days, we've watched two thousand girls perform. Most girls

were only concerned about their own performance, but not Mickey. She tried to ease her group's tension by making them laugh and in doing so, helped all of them to do a better job.'

I stop at the edge of the stage.

Sunshine grins. Johnny's mouth is twisted. It's hard to tell whether he's happy or cross.

"Mickey's a terrific talent, and a caring kid. We look forward to seeing more of her.'

I look out at the crowd and beam. There's nothing like the feeling of being applauded.

Jed winks at me as he takes center stage again.

"So ladies and gentlemen, that concludes the state auditions for Dream Diva. We hope you had us much fun as we did. We'll see you all next month on Dream Diva TV!"

Erin slips behind the others. "I told you!" She grins and hugs me.

"Sympathy vote," says Coco the Mini-Freak, plastic smile stuck to her face. "Neither of you will get any further than round two."

Erin and I look at each other and smile. "We'll see," I say, my arm around Erin's shoulder. "We'll see."

Going Solo

DIVA

Contents

Chapter One 63

Chapter Two 67

Chapter Three 70

Chapter Four 74

Chapter Five 78

Chapter Six 85

Chapter Seven 90

Chapter Eight 94

Chapter Nine 98

Chapter Ten 111

Chapter Eleven 114

Chapter One

I'm Mickey Farrell, youngest girl in a family of three. My sisters are sports-tragics. You name it and they not only play it, they win every trophy possible.

They dream of being sporting legends. I dream of being a singing star.

A month ago, I auditioned with 2,000 other girls at our state's auditions for Dream Diva. Today I'm flying north with my new friend, Erin Chang and Coco "Mini-Freak" Lamont to compete in round two of Diva. We're just three of the eight girls from our state that made it through.

Erin and I hit it off when we met at auditions. Erin's heaps of fun.

Mini-Freak's not so much fun. Sure, she has an amazing voice, but she's kind of painful. Before our flight even took off she complained because she didn't have a row to herself and couldn't put her feet up to stop her ankles swelling. Then she sent her breakfast back three times because the muffin was too cold, the juice too warm and the tray too dirty. And she insisted she be first off the plane.

Talk about annoying. But no way is she stopping me from giving Diva my best shot. After that meeting two weeks ago with the Diva officials, I know how tough round two is going to be.

It's going to take my very best to make my dreams come true.

At the meeting, the Diva team explained there are 25 girls competing for five final places. The 25 of us have been split into performing groups, with eight girls in Group One and Group Two and nine in Group Three. Erin, Mini-Freak and I are in Group Three. Each group will be singing live on *Diva TV*.

At first the group thing freaked me out. But once the officials explained *Diva TV* would go for five hours if we all sang on the one night, I was glad we'd been divided up.

Group One sang Wednesday night, Group Two on Friday night and our group performs Sunday night.

The officials also explained the judging. Basically it's a popularity contest. The judges' scores and the audience's votes combined decide four finalists.

The final spot is "judges' choice" and finalists can come from any group, maybe even all from the same one.

Before the meeting finished, we had to choose a song to perform from a list of 15. Talk about a tough choice. The songs are so old, Mom knew them. Lizzie, my

singing and dance teacher reckons the organizers pick old songs so we don't try to sing like today's pop stars.

I chose *Blame It On The Boogie*. It's pretty boppy, so the audience should get into it. With Lizzie's help, I funked it up and have been reworking it ever since.

At our last session yesterday, Lizzie gave me a small smiling Buddha statue. "Rub his belly for luck and believe in yourself, Mickey," she said.

That wasn't the only "lucky" gift I received yesterday. Last night my best friends, Hana and Charley, gave me the cutest frog pendant. Hana says frogs are lucky — the wider the mouth, the greater the fortune.

The Buddha will be in my pocket and my frog will be around my neck until round two is over. With 25 girls competing for five places, I need extra luck.

Chapter Two

The first person Mini-Freak, Erin and I see as the four-wheel drive parks in front of the exclusive Carringbush Hotel is Zoë Tamburo. "Good to see you girls."

Zoë was our supervisor at the Diva auditions. Just seeing her makes me feel relaxed. Not that I'm freaking out or anything. It's just that traveling without Mom and Dad is strange.

"Are you our supervisor again?" I ask.

"Sure am, Mickey," says Zoë.

"Fantastic!"

Zoë pats my shoulder. "Come meet the rest of your group."

"What about our luggage?" asks Coco.

"The staff will take it to your room."

We follow Zoë to the dining room, overlooking the pool.

"How cool is this?" says Erin.

"Seriously cool," I say.

"I've stayed in better," says Mini-Freak, checking her reflection in the glass doors.

Five other girls are waiting for us. One by one, we introduce ourselves.

Amara Bosisto and Jane Kelly have braces and live by the ocean, but on opposite sides of the country. Sky D'Angelo lives near the beach too and loves whales. Malak Ahmed's dad is a doctor in a small town. Darcy O'Sullivan shows cattle at agricultural shows. Liberty Winters lives in the city and rides a horse called Taffy at pony club. There's something familiar about Liberty.

Next, Zoë tells us who we're sharing rooms with.

"Hope I'm not sharing with Coco. Or Liberty. She keeps giving us weird looks," whispers Erin. She relaxes when Zoë pairs up Mini-Freak and Liberty. Erin ends up sharing with Malak and I'm sharing with Skye D'Angelo.

I so hope Skye's easy to talk to.

"You can go unpack, guys, but be back in 30 minutes for lunch,' says Zoë.

By the time Skye and I reach our room, we're nattering away about friends, school and the auditions.

We explore the room, checking out the balcony, flat screen TV and spa bath and help each other unpack.

"So," says Skye, sitting on my bed. "What's the deal with Coco?"

I sigh. "Who knows! She's a seriously good singer, but, well...you'll see."

Skye nods. "I think I already have." She glances at her watch. "Hey, we'd better go."

Chapter Three

By the pool, tables groan under piles of cold meats, salads and tropical fruit. My tummy rumbles as I choose chicken, pasta salad and beetroot.

Erin, Malak, Skye and I grab a table in the sun. Liberty and Mini-Freak join us.

"Great," mumbles Erin.

"Mic–ala," Coco's eyes sparkle. "You didn't tell us your father's a champion footballer."

"Is he?" asks Erin, eyes wide.

My face burns. How does she know my full name? And how does she know about Dad? "He retired five years ago."

Erin looks hurt. Coco is quick to pick up on it.

"Didn't you know, Erin? Micala never shuts up about him at school." Coco's smile is innocent — too innocent. "Or about her sisters being on the state swim team."

"It's not me who talks about them — it's Showbag, my P.E. teacher," I mumble. Only Showbag's not bragging about my family. He's picking on me. "Who'd guess your father is an elite athlete?" he says as I fumble a catch and "Funny — your sisters are on the state swim team and you can barely float".

Showbag is Ed McBride — Dog-Breath McBride's father. Dog-Breath is in my class at school. She's a major pain.

"Why Showbag?" Erin's face is hard to read.

"Because he's full of rubbish," I say.

Liberty drops her fork and glares at me. "That's horrible."

Zoë cruises over, folder in her hand. "Erin, Skye, Mickey, Coco and Liberty,

 **DIVA**

you're shopping after lunch. Malak, you and the rest of the group will be rehearsing. We'll meet in the foyer." Zoë zips across to the other table.

I shudder. "Wish she'd mix us up."

"Aren't we good enough?" Erin won't look at me.

I push my plate away and sigh.

When I first entered Dream Diva, my life went on as usual. Then *Diva TV* began.

At school, there are so many kids wanting to be my new best friends, Hana and Charley hang out without me.

Mr. Demitri, the principal, asks about Sunshine Harris all the time, and Mrs. Bolton doesn't hassle me about homework anymore. That's not a bad thing, but the effect it has on Dog-Breath McBride is.

Apart from constantly bumping my table, on Monday she "accidentally" deleted my space project from the class computers and I swear she was the one who glued my language book shut.

At least nothing's changed at home. Mom still goes off about my messy room and Dad still tells really bad jokes.

I rub my lucky frog pendant. With Mini-Freak knowing stuff about me and Erin being weird, I need all the help I can get.

Chapter Four

Cameraman Jerry and sound guy Zander film us climbing into one of the Diva four-wheel drives.

Liberty and Coco walk like they have rubber hips.

I raise my eyebrows at Erin.

She smiles back.

Maybe my frog pendant and Buddha are working.

On the way to Dobson's department store, Zoë explains the clothes are a gift from the store. "Pick three outfits. One for the performance Sunday night, another for the announcement Monday and a third for tomorrow's publicity."

Jerry and Zander race ahead filming as we weave through shoppers. People stare and point. Coco waves.

A woman with a ponytail pulled so tight she looks permanently surprised meets us at the Cool Chicks department. "Welcome to Dobson's — Exclusively Yours. I'm Natasha." She pronounces it "Nar-tar-shar".

Nar-tar-shar leads us past the sale rack to the designer section. I've never made it to this section before.

"Remember, three changes of clothes." Nar-tar-shar speaks like the Queen.

Erin and Skye race for dresses with rosebud prints.

"Too feminine for you, Micala?" says Mini-Freak.

"Try the boys' section," says Liberty.

Gritting my teeth, I go back to the sale rack to check out a yellow glitter top. It's my size so I take it with me.

In the designer section I pick out a purple halter top and skate pants.

"Great," says Nar-tar-shar, taking the purple top and pants. Her face twists at the yellow glitter top. "This is last season's."

"I like it."

Nar-tar-shar rolls her eyes. "Try it then."

The curtain flies open as I'm doing up the buttons on the purple pants. "Perfect." Nar-tar-shar spins me around. "Draws attention from your long neck."

Mini-Freak's laughter rings out. "Micala has a giraffe neck!"

Nar-tar-shar's eyes narrow. "Such an elegant neck." She disappears, returning with some seriously cool clothes. The funky dress reminds me of photos of Mom as a teenager, but my favorite is the summer version of the sale top.

"Gorgeous," says Nar-tar-shar every time I change.

Erin watches, face blank.

I decide on the purple top, skate pants, yellow summer top, black pants and the funky dress. Nar-tar-shar wraps them in silver tissue paper, slips them into bags and hands them to an assistant.

"There's a gift, too." Nar-tar-shar winks. "Don't let them drag you down."

She sails towards the shoe department where she selects two pairs of flats for me and a high, strappy pair that are "completely perfect" for the funky dress. I'd rather wear a flatter style, but Nar-tar-shar won't budge.

"What if the heel breaks?"

Nar-tar-shar taps the heel. "That will never happen."

"Even barefoot your dancing sucks," says Coco.

I'm about to tell Coco where I'd like to put my bare foot when Zoë says in her cheery way, "Time to go."

Chapter Five

Outside the TV studios, Diva flags flutter from flagpoles. Inside the foyer are Diva posters of host Jed Somerton, the judges and of the three groups.

"My hair's frizzy," says Skye, frowning at our poster.

"You look hot," I say, even though her hair is seriously frizzy.

Mini-Freak says, "You both need a stylist."

"Is that a zit?" I point to Coco's face on the poster.

"What?" She rushes over to examine it.

Zoë ushers us down a corridor lined with photographs of TV personalities to double doors printed with "Studio 2". Above is a red "ON AIR" sign.

"This," says Zoë, opening the door, "is the *Diva TV* studio."

My heart flutters. Glitz, action, glamour. My shoulders sag. The set is drab and empty.

"It's small," says Mini-Freak.

"This might help." Zoë hits a switch and the set is transformed.

Excitement surges through me. Tomorrow night, in my "completely perfect" shoes, I'll be singing right here.

Musicians stroll onto the set. The back-up singers slip into position.

"The judges sit at the front of the stage," says Zoë.

A bald guy dressed in black and a thin woman with gold rings on her spidery fingers strut across the stage.

"This is Hunter, our voice coach, and Mita, our choreographer. They work with

Sunshine and heaps of other stars," says Zoë, "and will be working with you."

Zoë and Mita sit in the judges' seats.

Hunter claps. "Circle ladies. Shoulders back, chests open." He has us doing breathing exercises, blowing raspberries and singing rounds.

"Terrific. Everyone except Mickey, take a seat."

I slip my hand in my pocket and rub Buddha's belly.

"*Boogie*, thanks." Hunter says to the band.

My heart goes crazy. I've sung with pianists, backing tapes and small orchestras, but never with a band and backing vocalists.

My first two lines are shaky.

"Stronger, Mickey," says Hunter.

I close my eyes and go for it.

Erin and Skye cheer when I finish.

Liberty and Mini-Freak scowl.

"Terrific, Mickey." Hunter hugs me, which is kind of weird. "Coco."

Mini-Freak brushes past. "Pathetic," she says.

"No, terrific," says Hunter, eyes narrowed.

Strawberry red, Coco sings *Circle of Life*.

Even though she sounds sensational, Hunter doesn't hug her.

Skye's *Girls Just Want to Have Fun* gets applause and a hug from Hunter.

Erin doesn't move while she sings *Twist and Shout*. Hunter pats her on the back.

Singing *Ring Ring*, Liberty dances like she needs to go to the toilet – urgently. Hunter pats her back too.

We spend the rest of Saturday afternoon working individually with Hunter, Mita and Zoë.

Hunter works on my breathing and

rhythm. Mita helps me use more of the stage. Zoë teaches me how to use the microphone properly and how to sing to the camera.

Before we finish, Zoë announces our singing order. "And so you know, we pulled your names out of a bowl. The order is random."

Coco sings first, then me, Liberty, Skye, Erin, Darcy, Jane, Amara and Malak is last. I'm exhausted and starving by the time we scramble back into the four-wheel drive.

"Tomorrow's publicity is organized," says Zoë, slipping her phone into her bag. "Malak, Darcy and Jane will do *Cool As* radio. Skye, Erin and Amara will be interviewed for tomorrow's newspaper at MegaFun Park..."

Guess who I'm with!

"...and Coco, Liberty and Mickey are on *Wicked*."

Liberty squeals.

Wicked is the coolest TV show. Hana, Charley and I never miss it, and it's the only non-sport show The Tragics watch. Actually, the only non-sporting posters in their rooms are *Wicked* hosts Kandy and Mack.

"You're so lucky," says Skye.

Erin stares out the window.

"Grab your shopping bags," says Zoë, as we park outside the Carringbush. "Dinner's at 7:00 with Jed and the judges."

In my room, I rummage through my bags for Nar-tar-shar's gift. It's the yellow sale top with a note.

"Ignore those two, Mickey. Enjoy the shirt, love Natasha."

There's a knock at our unit door.

It's Mini-Freak.

"Zoë asked me to tell you dinner's at 7:15 now."

 DIVA

"Why didn't she tell us?" asks Skye, standing behind me.

Coco shrugs and turns to go. "Oh, and wear your pajamas."

"Pajamas?"

Mini-Freak nods. "It's a pajama party." She trots to the elevator.

Chapter Six

"It's quiet," I say as Skye, wearing Tweety PJs, and me, in Snoopy pajamas, stroll down the corridor.

"Maybe we're early." Skye opens the dining room door.

Actually, we're late.

Johnny Mawton stands at the front of the room, addressing everyone.

"Let's bolt," I whisper.

"Interesting choice of clothes, girls." Johnny's voice is cold.

Too late!

Jerry points his camera at us.

Laughter bounces off the walls. Liberty and Coco laugh the hardest. Erin, sitting with them, chews her thumb.

Liberty mouths "Gotcha".

A rushing sound fills my ears.

"C'mon," whispers Skye, strolling to Johnny.

Teeth gritted, I follow.

"Thought we'd lift the tension, Johnny. I mean, Diva is meant to be fun." Skye smiles sweetly.

"Exactly," I say, finding my voice. "Why do it if it's not fun?"

"Yes, fun." Johnny screws up his nose. "Take a seat, girls."

We bolt towards the first empty chairs we see.

"I'll kill Coco," hisses Skye.

"She set you up, didn't she?" Zoë's eyes blaze.

Mini-Freak's joke has backfired. We're sharing a table with Zoë and Jed.

"You covered it well," says Jed.

"But Johnny..." Skye's face is white. So much for confident Skye.

"I'll handle Johnny," says Zoë.

"Where was I?" says Johnny before launching into the story of his TV career. Instead of listening, I stew over what to say to Mini-Freak and Liberty.

Johnny finishes and dinner is served.

Chicken stuffed with sundried tomatoes, honey carrots and creamy potatoes. Seriously yum.

While we eat, Jed tells us stories about he and his little brother riding motorbikes on his family farm.

After chocolate mousse and strawberries for dessert, Sunshine and Gwen join us. Gwen tells us about being in a rock band in the 90s. Swearing us to secrecy, Sunshine tells us her character in *Misty Beach* is getting married next season.

Across the room Mini-Freak's face is the color of an eggplant. She's dead-set about to explode with anger. Her plan

to make Skye and I look like idiots has totally backfired. Thanks to Mini-Freak, Skye and I know Zoë and Jed even better.

At 9:30, Jed strolls to the front and explains tomorrow's schedule. Publicity first, rehearsals at the studios, and then the show. Once we're done, we have dinner with our families, who fly in tomorrow afternoon. "Bring tomorrow night's clothes to the foyer in the morning Divas, and sleep well."

"PJs are so comfy," says Skye, while we wait for the lift.

Mini-Freak saunters up with Liberty. Erin stands behind them. Before I can speak, Coco snarls, "Sitting with Jed doesn't make you hot, Micala. Hot people don't cry because they can't do high jump."

Liberty sniggers.

How does she know this stuff? What if she finds out about my underwear tragedy? "I was crying because my grandfather had died."

Behind them, Erin fidgets with her bracelet. The lift opens. I shove Skye inside and the doors close.

"They're warped," says Skye.

"Mini-Freak and Liberty are. Erin's not like them."

Before I go to bed, I ring home. Dad answers and I tell him everything – the pajamas, Mini-Freak knowing stuff and Erin being weird.

"Mickey, some people are so desperate to win, they play dirty," says Dad. "Just be yourself. And if it gets worse we'll set The Tragics on them."

I'm all talked out when Mom takes the phone, but that doesn't stop her asking if I'm eating properly.

Exhausted, I crawl into bed. Hopefully my Buddha and frog on the bedside table will rain luck on me while I sleep.

Chapter Seven

Clothes for tonight across my arm, frog around my neck and Buddha stuffed in my skate pants pocket; I'm ready for the day.

In the foyer, Zander and Jerry race around filming.

A girl wearing a Diva T-shirt takes my clothes. Zoë directs everyone to the waiting four-wheel drives.

Coco and Liberty strut ahead.

I'm relieved when Zoë climbs into our car. "*Wicked* is filmed at the same studios as Diva," she says.

When we arrive, we go straight to make-up where Liberty and Coco fire instructions at the make-up girls.

"More blush."

"My hair's flat."

Wicked hosts, Kandy and Mack, stroll into the room and Zoë introduces us.

Mack leans against the mirrors. "This'll be pretty relaxed."

"Yep, just a chat between friends," says Kandy, who's even prettier than she looks on TV.

"I'll be spokesperson," says Coco.

Zoë clears her throat.

"Thanks, but we'll talk to all of you," says Kandy.

"All good," says Mack, rubbing his chin. "See you on set."

The Interview

Kandy: *How lucky are we, Mack? We have three very talented divas with us today. Welcome Mickey Farrell, Coco Lamont and Liberty Winters.*

Mack: *Mickey, is Dream Diva fun?*

Mickey: *It's the best. New friends, being on* Wicked, *singing and dancing — I love it.*

Kandy: *Isn't it scary singing in front of the judges, Coco?*

Coco: *Well, I'm very experienced, so it doesn't worry me. Others struggle.*

Mack: *Is it hard being the last group to face the judges?*

Liberty: *It's no different, except we sing Sunday night.*

Mickey: *No matter what, you still get nervous.*

Coco: *Mickey's inexperienced, so it's overwhelming for her. I've been performing since I was two—*

Kandy: *Is it tough travelling without your parents?*

Mickey: *I miss them, but our supervisor Zoë is terrific.*

Liberty: *Micala and I are lucky. My uncle teaches at her school and my cousin is her friend.*

Kandy: *So you know each other?*

Liberty: *Really well.*

Mack: *That must help, Mickey.*

Mickey: *Pardon?*

Mack: *Knowing Liberty must be good.*

Mickey: *Ummm...*

Kandy: *How are the judges, Coco?*

Coco: *Sensational, especially Johnny. He really knows his stuff.*

Mack: *And I guess there are lots of laughs too.*

Liberty: *You bet! Mickey cracked us up on the way here. She told us how she came back from the school toilet with her dress tucked into her underpants.*

Mickey: *What?*

Kandy: *Why don't we take a look at the girls performing?*

Mack: *Cool! Remember you have 24 hours to vote for your favorite after tonight's show.*

Kandy: *Thanks Liberty and Coco. Good luck, Mickey!*

Chapter Eight

Could it be any worse?

My underwear tragedy broadcast on national TV, and I find out Liberty is Dog-Breath's cousin and Showbag's niece.

"You didn't tell Liberty that story did you?" whispers Zoë, as I step off the set.

I shake my head.

"At least they don't have photos." Zoë smiles. "It happened to me at a press conference once."

That makes me feel better. "I wish Liberty and I weren't in the same group."

Zoë sighs. "So do I."

I guess it's not all bad. At least I know where Mini-Freak's been getting her information. And if I can stand up to Dog-Breath, I can stand up to Liberty Winters.

Mini-Freak, Liberty and I watch the rest of *Wicked* from backstage, then eat lunch with Mack and Kandy in the shabby cafeteria. Mack warns us about the food, but my pizza and strawberry shake taste great.

Before the rest of our group arrives, Kandy and Mack sign posters and T-shirts for us and for The Tragics, Hana and Charley.

After lunch, our entire group runs through tonight's show again and again. Hunter and Mita offer advice. The judges sip coffee and watch.

Skye is easily the best. Poor Malak struggles with her pitch and sounds awful. I ignore Liberty and Mini-Freak's dirty looks while I sing. After the third run-through, we gather around Hunter, Mita, floor manager Declan, and Zoë.

"Terrific, girls. Remember tonight, no matter what, keep going," says Zoë.

"I'd like to see more razzle dazzle," calls Johnny.

Zoë cuts him off. "Time to get ready."

I nearly freak out when I realize I'm sharing a dressing room with Coco, Liberty and Erin. I stick to the corner until Coco and Liberty rush to make-up.

My dress is impossible to do up on my own. "Erin, could you help, please?"

Erin nods. "Done." She sniffs.

I face her. "Are you okay?"

"I'm…" Her voice is squeaky. "Mickey, when Coco knew that stuff, I was hurt. I thought we were friends."

"We are… at least I thought we were."

"You're so good and I'm—" She shrugs. "I'm sorry for—"

"Forget it, Erin. Let's go to make-up." I pick up my shoes and put them down again. "I'll grab these on the way back."

"It's revolting!" screeches Mini-Freak.

Coco's hair falls in soft ringlets.

"It looks great," I say.

Coco eyes drip poison. "Don't be sarcastic."

"She's not," says Erin. "It's beautiful."

Coco glares at her reflection.

I jump into a chair and let make-up artist Kitty work. By the time she's done I hardly recognize myself.

"Mickey, you look hot," says Erin.

When Erin and I return to the dressing room, Liberty's standing in the doorway. "We have to go."

"I need my shoes," I say, squeezing past.

Weird, but my shoes aren't where I left them. I shrug and slip them on.

Chapter Nine

In the Green Room, a *Diva TV* ad plays on a flat screen TV. Coco beaming. Liberty singing. Me laughing. My stomach flips.

Everyone's quiet and focused, except for Mini-Freak. She's more sulky than focused.

When Johnny, Sunshine and Gwen arrive the scowl slips from Coco's face.

"Coco, your hair's fabulous," says Johnny.

Coco flicks a ringlet. "Thank you."

Skye pretends to vomit.

"Have fun, everyone," says Sunshine.

"Remember, razzle dazzle," says Johnny.

Razzle dazzle? If my stomach wasn't flipping out so much, I'd laugh.

Jed bops into the room. "Wow! You guys look gorgeous." He clicks his fingers. "Let's go."

Zoë waits at the edge of the set, folder in hand.

I crane my neck looking for my family, but it's impossible to see.

The *Diva TV* theme starts. Jed jogs onto the set. The crowd claps and cheers.

"Let's meet Group Three." Jed clicks and winks up a storm. "Please welcome Coco Lamont..."

Coco fluffs her ringlets and struts through the gap.

"...Mickey Farrell..."

I take a deep breath and walk onto the stage.

The lights and noise are seriously scary. I wave and stand beside Coco.

The first people I see in the crowd are

Showbag and Dog-Breath. My stomach just about leaps out of my mouth.

Two rows in front of them, The Tragics hold a "Mickey Rocks" poster. Mom and Dad wave.

Once everyone's on stage, Jed explains the scoring. "So, the judges" scores combined with the audience votes for all 25 girls will be tallied to decide our four finalists. The judges choose the fifth finalist. You never know, all five finalists could be from tonight's group." Jed double clicks at the camera. "We'll meet our first Diva from Group Three, Coco Lamont, after the break."

The *Diva TV* theme combined with the audience's roar nearly knocks me over.

"Coco, stay there. Mickey, wait in the wings," says Zoë. "Everyone else to the Green Room."

"You're out of here, Micala," hisses Liberty.

"Let's keep those vocal chords loose," says Hunter.

While Mini-Freak sings, we pull faces and hum. It's actually relaxing.

"Okay, Mickey," says Zoë.

Hunter hugs me. "Watch your breathing. And have fun!"

Coco breezes past. "Hope you can handle those shoes, Micala."

Weirdo! I ignore her.

Zoë hands me a microphone and nudges me forward.

The applause hits me like a wave.

I take slow breaths.

The band plays the introduction.

Cameras zoom towards me.

The audience seems to be moving closer.

My stomach knots. My brain screams.

"Breathe."

"Watch your pitch."

"Relax!"

Just when I think I'm about to lose it, the music fills me from my fingers to my toes. I'm singing and using the whole stage, just like Mita taught me.

The kids in the front row clap and sing. Mom, Dad and The Tragics stand and dance. Everything's fantastic until my left leg collapses. I stumble, fighting for balance. I look down. My "completely perfect" heel has fallen off.

I stop singing. The band keeps playing.

I stare at the crowd. Mom looks horrified. Behind her, Dog-Breath laughs.

I toss both shoes and the heel behind me.

Eyes closed, I refocus and pick up the beat.

I've only missed a line and a half.

I start singing again. The crowd roars. Barefoot, I sing and dance, trying not to think about what just happened.

Before I know it, my song's finished.

I can hardly hear Jed over the cheers and applause.

"Sensational effort, Mickey. Are you okay?"

"I'm fine, but I think my shoe is dead."

Jed and the audience laugh. "Why *Blame It On The Boogie*?"

"It's a fun song and I wanted the audience to enjoy it."

"Sounds like they did. Did you?"

"Yeah! I did."

"Well, let's see what the judges thought."

It feels like my stomach is filled with jittering bugs.

The spotlight hits Gwen. "Mickey, you have a fantastic voice and your bright personality shines through when you perform. You handled a disaster beautifully. A fantastic job. 18 out of 20."

The crowd cheers. I can't help but smile. Sunshine stands and claps when the spotlight hits her. "Mickey, what an effort. I've seen performers twice your age toss it in after something like that. But you kept going. You have a huge future — 18."

"Thanks, Sunshine."

The spotlight moves to Johnny. Why does he only frown at me? I wipe my palms on my dress.

Johnny taps the desk with his pen. "Your pitch was passable, but your dancing's so bad you broke your shoe."

I bite my lip. I knew he'd be tough, but this is cruel.

"Rubbish." Sunshine's face is red.

A hush falls over the crowd.

"I call it as I see it."

"Well, clearly, you need glasses," says Gwen, arms folded.

The audience cheers.

Johnny straightens his tie.

"No razzle. No dazzle. Not a patch on Coco — 5."

Sunshine buries her face in her hands. Gwen looks like she might hit someone. The crowd boos.

"That's 41 points, Mickey. Do you have anything to say about Johnny's comments?"

I swallow, trying to move the lump in my throat. "It's cool. I gave it my best."

The clapping and cheering hurts my ears.

"Our audience loves you, Mickey."

"Thanks, Jed. Thanks everyone."

Jed places his arm on my shoulder.

"After the break, Liberty Winters."

The *Diva TV* theme fills the room. The lights fade. I breathe out noisily.

"Johnny sucks," says Jed.

"No, I stuffed up." I trudge off stage.

Zoë hands me the shoes and heel. "Mickey, this was no accident."

"It doesn't matter, now."

Hunter holds my face. "Mickey, I'm so sorry."

"Like the present from me and my cousin?" asks Liberty, smirking.

I gasp. It all makes sense. My shoes in a different place after make-up. Mini-Freak's comment. My shoe falling apart.

"You wrecked my shoe."

Liberty's laugh is shrill.

Now Hunter gasps. "No!"

"I knew it," says Zoë, standing with Jed. Their faces are dark like storm clouds. Jed shakes his head and walks away.

"We'll sort this out later." Zoë's mouth is a thin line. "Liberty, on stage."

"Are you okay?" asks Erin, when I return to the Green Room.

"I can't believe you kept going!" Skye hands me a juice.

Mita pats my shoulder. "Johnny was horrible."

"He's just honest," says Mini-Freak, still fluffing her ringlets.

"That's enough, Coco," says Mita.

The ad break ends and everyone gathers around the TV. I stand behind the couches to watch, but can't stop thinking about Johnny's comments and Liberty sabotaging my shoe.

I miss Liberty's performance, but manage to focus on Erin, who struggles with her rhythm, and Skye, who's amazing. Once we've all sung, Zoë hustles us back to the set.

Jed repeats the scores. Skye leads with 57 points. Coco is second with 53, Amara has 50 and Darcy and Jane tie on 49. Malak scores 48 and Erin 46. Liberty, who barely moved when she sang, scores 43. And the lowest score? Me, with 41.

Balloons and confetti drop from the ceiling. We wave and kick the balloons. Liberty, face white, stands apart from us.

"Clear," yells Declan over the noise.

Zoë herds us off stage. "Your families will meet us in the cafeteria."

Instead of drab grey, the cafeteria's now pink, silver and spectacular. Pink tablecloths, pink and silver helium balloons and silver candles. And the food smells yum. I've just found our table when Mom, Dad and The Tragics burst through the door.

"You were way cool," says Gemma.

"You made Dad cry," says Sam.

"Hayfever." Dad winks. "We're proud of you."

"That man is an idiot," says Mom, wrapping an arm around my shoulder.

I figure she's talking about Johnny.

"So what happened?" asks Dad.

By the time I've finished explaining, Mom looks like she's about to explode.

Dad's eyes go weird. "And Zoë is sorting it out?"

"Looks like it," I say, nodding at Liberty's mom and Showbag talking to Zoë and a guy in a suit.

While we eat, I tell my family about Nar-Tar-Shar, *Wicked* and Erin.

After the plates are cleared, Gwen, Sunshine and Jed pull chairs up to our table and rave about my performance. Embarrassing! When Kandy and Mack join us for chocolate cheesecake, Gemma nearly passes out. Sam flutters her eyelashes. Dad leaves to talk to Zoë.

"Zoë reckons you've been terrific," says Dad, sitting back down.

"Of course." I grin. "What's happening?"

"Liberty's admitted to everything," says Dad. "Her uncle caused trouble when we played football together, too."

"You played football with Showbag?" I squeak.

Dad shrugs. "He only lasted a year."

"What happens to Liberty?" asks Mom.

"She has to explain everything to Sunshine, Gwen and Johnny and apologize to them and Mickey."

"So she should!" It's not like Mom to be so hard.

Jed jumps onto a chair and whistles. "You were sensational, girls. How about a day off at the zoo tomorrow?"

We cheer and stamp our feet.

"We'll meet your families there at 10:00 a.m. Before we finish up, let's congratulate Mickey Farrell on her courage tonight."

Everyone stands and claps. It's kind of embarrassing, but it feels good. Snuggled in my bed, I try to focus on the good stuff instead of the shoe thing and Johnny's comments. I toss and turn but eventually, with the Buddha and frog on the bedside table, I fall asleep.

Chapter Ten

At breakfast, Liberty sits alone. Coco shares a table with Malak and Amara.

"What's with those two?" asks Skye.

I shrug. No way am I saying Liberty wrecked my shoe. Zoë can tell them.

A bunch of flowers walks towards me. Actually, there's a girl carrying it, but the arrangement is so big that all I can see is her legs.

Skye hands me the card. "Read it."

"Dear Mickey, good luck tonight, love Natasha and the Dobson's staff."

Next, a delivery guy brings a big purple teddy from Gwen and Sunshine, a huge box of chocolates from Kandy and Mack and a stack of CDs from Jed.

"I wish *my* shoe broke," says Erin.

After breakfast, Skye helps me carry everything to our room except for the chocolates. I share those with everyone on the way to the zoo.

When we arrive, our families are waiting for us by the main gate. Beside them are heaps of journalists.

Microphones are thrust at us as we step off the bus.

"Mickey, were you hurt last night?"

"Tell us the toilet story."

Zoë tucks me under her arm and cuts a path to the gate. "Just smile at them," she tells me.

Once we're inside, my family and I tour the zoo. Gemma calls a grumpy chimpanzee Liberty and at the petting zoo a rabbit bites Dad's finger.

Everyone meets up again at the zoo café for lunch – fish and chips, salads and the biggest ice cream cones. I stay away from Liberty and Mini-Freak and their families.

After lunch, we do publicity by the lions' enclosure, then it's a "behind the scenes" tour. Skye, Erin and I feed the seals and hold a python. We all cuddle Liberty the chimpanzee, only her real name is Peppy.

Suddenly it's four o'clock and time to go.

Mom swallows me in a bear hug. "No matter what, we love you, Mickey."

I wriggle out of her grip, only to have Dad swoop on me.

"We're proud of you, Mick."

When The Tragics step forward, I sprint for the mini-bus.

I stick my head out the window, wave and blow kisses.

Not long now till I find out if my dreams might still come true.

Chapter Eleven

The girls from the other two groups are on the set when we arrive. Jed, Declan and Zoë run us through tonight's program.

"Walk out and take a seat, then we'll play a video of your performances. Okay?" asks Declan.

We nod.

"Cool," says Zoë. "Go change. Your clothes are in your dressing rooms."

This time I share a dressing room with Amara, Skye, Erin and Malak. After we're changed and made-up, we head for the Green Room.

It's a relief when the couches are full. There's no telling what my squirming stomach will do if I sit down.

Knees jiggling, I lean against the wall.

Beside me Erin chews her thumb. Skye stares at the television. Liberty, wedged in the corner of the couch, taps her feet. Mini-Freak flicks through a *Girls Stuff* magazine.

"Group One," says Zoë.

My heart thuds in my throat.

The *Diva TV* theme blasts out of the television speakers.

Jed chats, clicks and winks. Group One fills the back row of seats on the stage.

I flatten myself against the wall as Group Two files out. I want to say good luck, but I'm too scared to open my mouth in case my heart splats against the opposite wall.

And then it's our turn.

My hearts thuds harder. My stomach's like a gymnast on parallel bars.

Liberty slinks past, head low.

In the wings, I take deep breaths.

The Diva theme soars.

Jed introduces Coco.

"Good luck, Mickey," says Zoë, squeezing my hand.

Jed calls my name.

The cheer's deafening. Blushing, I wave and trot to my seat in the front row, next to Coco.

Once we're all seated, the film clips of our performances roll.

No way am I looking. I know how ridiculous I felt. I don't need to see it.

Jed claps when the clips finish. "Give it up for Group Three."

The audience claps, hoots and whistles.

Jed clicks and points. "And now we'll announce our finalists — right after the break."

The audience groans. I groan too.

During the ad break, Declan hands Jed a pink and silver envelope.

Jed jogs across the studio to five funky chairs.

The *Diva TV* theme soars.

As if my heart and stomach aren't enough, now my teeth chatter and my ears buzz. I'm about to explode!

The lights come up. The contents of my stomach nearly do, too.

"Welcome back to *Diva TV*." Jed flashes his best smile. "Let's find out who our finalists are. Remember, the group the girls performed with plays no part in deciding which of our 25 girls are finalists. The four finalists are decided by combining the judges' scores with the audience votes. The judges alone decide the fifth finalist. Now, let's find out who our finalists are."

Jed opens the envelope. "Our first finalist, from Group One, is Mai Tran..."

Mai squeals and sprints to the first chair.

"...from Group Two, Imogen Beckworth."

Imogen pumps the air, kisses Jed and sits beside Mai.

"...from Group Three..."

Maybe, just maybe.

Mini-Freak's knuckles are white.

"...Skye D'Angelo."

I whistle and cheer.

"And our fourth finalist, from Group Three is..."

"Me," says Mini-Freak, uncrossing her legs.

I stare at my jiggling knees.

"...Coco Lamont."

I swallow the lump in my throat, which is probably my no-longer-beating heart. "Well done, Coco."

She smooths her skirt and strolls to the fourth chair.

The air rushes from me.

No way will I be the judges' choice, not

after last night. Anyway, Johnny hates me.

"One empty seat, 21 girls," says Jed walking over to we rejects. "Our last finalist in a moment."

During the break, Jed flops into Mini-Freak's empty seat. "This sucks, Mickey. You have more viewer votes than Imogen and Coco."

If he's trying to make me feel better, it's not working.

"Doesn't matter, Jed. I've had fun."

Beside me, Liberty wriggles in her seat.

Jed pats my knee and jogs to the finalists. Mini-Freak looks like she's just eaten the last chocolate chip cookie.

Applause and the *Diva TV* music fill my head.

Erin shuffles across to Mini-Freak's now-empty seat. "You'll make it, Mickey."

I shake my head. "I stuffed it."

"I'm sorry, Mickey," says a small voice to my left.

At first I think I've imagined it. I glance at Liberty and know I've heard right. A tear slips down her cheek.

"Time to find out who's the fifth finalist." Jed does his biggest click and pistol point.

I glance at Mom and Dad. They mouth "I love you".

My body has stopped flipping, jittering and thudding. I know my Diva dream is over.

The spotlight shines on Gwen.

"Our decision is based not only on last night's performance, but on what our voice coach, choreographer and supervisors say. One girl stands out, not only for her talent, but for the way she behaves and treats others. The decision was easy for Sunshine and me. Johnny took longer, but he's an old stick-in-the-mud."

The crowd laughs.

Johnny bows.

Gwen clears her throat. "It gives me enormous pleasure to announce our fifth finalist…"

A rumble starts from the back of the audience, rolling forward like a wave until it's a chant.

"Mickey. Mickey. Mickey."

My mouth drops open.

Gwen raises her hands. The chant fades away. It was nice while it lasted.

"The fifth finalist is Mickey Farrell."

The crowd goes completely crazy!

Erin leaps to her feet, screaming.

Sunshine, Gwen and Johnny stand and clap.

"Me?" I say, looking from them to Jed.

Jed, clapping like crazy, nods. "You!"

A smile crawls across my face. I jog across to the final, funky seat.

Skye hugs me.

Mini-Freak smiles, but her eyes are like ice. "Sympathy vote, Micala."

"Whatever, Coco." No way is she spoiling this.

Streamers and confetti rain upon us. All around me are smiling faces. Even Johnny shakes my hand.

The *Diva TV* theme becomes louder and it's all over.

The best hug of all is from my family. I made it! Only more step to become the Dream Diva.

I stroke Lizzie's Buddha in my pocket. To win the final is going to be hard work and I will need all the luck I can get!

Contents

Chapter One 129

Chapter Two 133

Chapter Three 138

Chapter Four 142

Chapter Five 147

Chapter Six 150

Chapter Seven 154

Chapter Eight 158

Chapter Nine 171

Chapter Ten 174

Chapter Eleven 177

Glossary 192

Quiz One...194

Quiz Two...197

Answers 200

Chapter One

I'm Mickey Farrell, youngest girl in a family of three. My sisters are sports-tragics. You name it and they not only play it, but they win every trophy possible.

They dream of being sporting legends. I dream of being a singing star.

Two months ago I auditioned for Diva, along with 2,000 other girls from my state. Tonight I'm competing against Mai Tran, Imogen Beckworth, Coco "Mini-Freak" Lamont and my friend Skye D'Angelo in the Diva Finale at Wonderland, the country's biggest theme park.

 **DIVA**

Even though I arrived at the Seaview International Hotel before nine this morning, I haven't seen the other girls. It's been too crazy.

My day started with rehearsals. First with choreographer Mita, then on to voice-coach Hunter and the band. I had a short break for a creamy pasta lunch in my room with Mom. After lunch, Nar-Tar-Shar from Dobson's Exclusively Yours dropped in. I had to choose clothes for tonight's performance and tomorrow night's show from the amazing outfits she'd brought with her. And then I moved on to having my hair and make-up done by make-up artist Kitty.

At least everything's set up at the Seaview International. We don't travel anywhere until tonight's show and we leave for that in 45 minutes.

Right now, while I wait in my room for Nar-Tar-Shar to bring the clothes

I've selected, Mom's showering. It's cool having Mom here. The Diva organizers insisted we have a parent with us this time. No one's saying why, but I bet it's because Liberty went crazy during Round Two.

Dad and The Tragics are staying at a hotel up the road. I'll see them after tonight's show.

There's a tap at the door.

Nar-Tar-Shar, arms full of Dobson bags, air-kisses my cheeks. "Mickey, your hair is divine."

She helps me into the cropped denim pants and pink tee-shirt printed with a silver guitarist so I don't mess up my hair and make-up. She even helps me with the beaded shoes, the silver bracelets, chunky necklace and matching earrings.

"Fabulous, Mickey," says Nar-Tar-Shar, when I'm dressed.

I lift the chunky necklace.

"Not too OTT?"

"OTT?" asks Mom, standing in the doorway.

"Over The Top," explains Nar-Tar-Sha. "And no Mickey, it's TP — Totally Perfect."

"She's right, Mickey. You look fantastic," says Mom, who is totally biased.

I grab my board shorts from the floor and reach into the pocket. "Nar-Tar-Shar, my friends Hana and Charley gave me this. He's lucky." I hold out the wide-mouth frog necklace. "Do you think—"

"How darling!" Nar-Tar-Shar clips it around my neck. "Not that you need luck." She air-kisses my cheeks, again. "Time you joined the others in Room 101."

Chapter Two

My heart's thudding when I walk into Room 101.

Mai, Imogen and their respective moms chat by the glass doors. Skye's mom brushes fluff off Skye's black halter dress.

"Mickey!" squeals Skye, dress swishing as she runs towards me. Her hair's held back with a glittering headband, and black earrings hang to her shoulders.

"You look sensational!" I say, feeling better just for seeing her.

Skye was kind of unsure when I first met her, but now she's different. Not bad different, just straighter, happier. More confident, I guess.

Skye introduces us to her mom, Anne. Anne's nothing like I expected. No flowing skirts or masses of earrings, just white pants, a lemon cross-over top and silver hoop earrings.

"What are you singing?" asks Skye, leading me to a table filled with sandwiches, cans of drinks and bowls of lollipops.

"*Walking On Sunshine*. What about you?"

"*I Can See Clearly Now*." Skye grabs a tomato sandwich. "Hunter talked me into a change of pace.

"How cool was it working with Hunter and Mita at home?" Hunter and Mita spent two days with each of us and our singing and dancing teachers last week.

Skye's eyes flash. "Way cool! I learned so much."

Mini-Freak and her mom stride into

the room. I can't decide if Mini-Freak's dress is green with a white print or white with a green print.

Mini-Freak's smile is more a sneer. "You look relaxed, Micala."

"Thanks, Coco. I feel it."

Mini-Freak scoffs. "I'm not talking about your feelings, Micala. I am talking about your clothes. Going on a family drive?"

Zoë rushes through the door before I can answer.

"Hi everyone. We won't have time for dinner before the show, so grab a bite to eat while we chat," says Zoë. "First, the limos will take you to the theatre stage door—"

"No red carpet?" says Coco.

"No, Coco. We're trying to keep it low key."

"Will the media be at the stage door?" Coco's mom says "stage door" the same

way most people say "garbage bin".

"They don't know exactly when or where the girls arrive. The girls are under enough pressure, Libby, without that attention." Zoë's smile is different from usual — kind of not a smile at all. "At the theatre, we'll run through the show and rehearse with the band. Questions?"

"How big is the theatre?" asks Mai.

"About the same size as the TV studio."

Imogen sticks her hand in the air, as though she's at school. "How many people will be there?"

"More than last time, but you won't see them because of the lights."

"Who sings first?" Imogen's voice is all sing-song, like a really little kid. .

"Skye's first, then Coco, Mai, Imogen and Mickey."

"And is voting the same as last time?" asks Mini-Freak.

"Exactly. The judges' scores will be combined with viewer votes."

Coco smirks at me. "No judges' choice?"

My face burns.

Across the room, Mom folds her arms.

Zoë's eyes flash. "Keep it nice, Coco."

"That's harsh, Zoë." Libby Lamont looks offended. "Coco's just asking a question."

Zoë sighs. "Let's just keep everything positive, okay? Finally, please keep your limousine windows up at all times. We'd like to keep how terrific you look a surprise." She rubs her hands together. "Let's go."

Chapter Three

Mini-Freak struts to the first of five limousines parked behind a Diva four-wheel drive. Imogen skips to the second limo. Mai climbs into the third.

I nudge Skye towards the next one and walk with Mom to the last limousine.

The uniformed driver opens the door. "Welcome, ladies."

I gasp. Leather seats, sunroof, TV, CD and DVD, fridge and a glass cupboard. I slide inside, grab the remote and start clicking buttons. The TV turns on, the sunroof opens and a CD plays.

"You're as bad as your dad," says Mom, taking the remote from me.

"Wait till Erin, Hana and Charley find out I've been in a limo."

I miss Erin. We've been friends since auditions and still email and phone each other, even after she was voted out in Round Three.

I rub my lucky frog's belly.

"Nervous?" asks Mom.

"A bit. My stomach's jumpy."

The limousine turns into the Wonderland entrance.

People are lined up outside the theatre's main door. Beside them, journalists and camera crews wait, microphones and cameras at the ready.

My stomach goes from jumpy to seriously flipping out.

"So much for keeping the windows up." says Mom, nodding at the first limousine.

Mini-Freak's leaning out the window, waving and blowing kisses.

Suddenly the media gathered at the

front of the theatre swarms around the side of the building. By the time our limo stops, there is a wall of photographers, camera crews, and journalists in front of the stage door.

So much for secrecy.

The window between us and the driver opens. "Zoë will tell you when to go."

"Let me guess," says Mom. "Someone tipped them off."

"Lead limo apparently."

Zoë jumps out of the Diva four-wheel drive and marches towards the media.

"Why aren't they arriving at the front?" asks a guy in a suit.

Zoë folds her arms. "These are kids, not seasoned celebrities. Let's give them space."

"Zoë, Coco's very experienced," calls out Libby Lamont. "I'm happy for her to be interviewed."

A muscle twitches in Zoë's jaw.

"That's not a problem, is it?" says Libby.

"Fine," says Zoë. "But the others are not to be photographed, filmed or interviewed."

Mini-Freak steps smiling from her limousine and the media bustles towards her.

Zoë waves us out of the cars.

As Mom and I reach the stage door, Coco's voice booms out. "The other girls aren't handling the pressure at all."

"Is she always like that?" asks Mai.

"She's usually worse," says Skye.

"Green Room's to your right," says Zoë, holding the door.

Chapter Four

"This is so exciting," says Imogen, lying across one of the four sofas in the green room.

"Exciting? Scary," says Mai. "If I don't take this herbal stuff I vomit and everything."

"How big is that TV?" says Skye, nodding to the enormous flat screen TV. On either side of a door marked "STAGE" is a keyboard and a table holding more food, bottles of drink, mini chocolate bars and mints. The way my stomach is churning, no way will I be going anywhere near it.

Diva TV host, Jed, wearing jeans and a suit jacket, strolls in with floor manager, Declan.

"You look stunning," says Jed, winking and finger clicking already. "And you kids don't look too bad either."

Mom giggles.

"Ready to go?" asks Declan.

"Not quite," says Zoë. "Coco's holding a press conference outside."

Jed laughs. "There's a surprise."

Declan checks his watch. "We can't wait."

Libby gushes into the room. "Zoë, Coco performed beautifully."

"Terrific," says Zoë in a voice that sounds like she doesn't think it's terrific. "Let's go. Moms, you can watch from the wings."

Backstage, there are heaps of cables, sets and people rushing about, just like a TV studio. On stage, it's different. There's a balcony in the auditorium, padded seats instead of rows of plastic chairs and the set's heaps bigger.

My mouth goes dry.

"Are we meant to use the whole stage?" asks Mia, wringing her hands.

"Just the middle." Zoë leads us to the front of the stage. "See, the set's divided into three sections. The judges sit to the right, Jed works from the left and you guys sing in the center, in front of the band."

"Have a walk around, then we'll rehearse," says Declan.

I stumble as I take a step.

"Shoe problem, Micala?" Coco brushes past me to center stage, where she and Libby, step out the set.

Skye, Mai and I explore and chat to the band.

"Gather round, girls," yells Declan, after a few minutes.

He walks us through the program twice, then watches from the front of the stage, yelling advice while we practice with Jed.

Jed doesn't wink or click until Declan declares we're ready.

"Great job, guys!" says Jed, practically exploding with clicks and winks.

Over Jed's shoulder I notice the judges, Gwen, Sunshine and Johnny, and Hunter and Mita watching in the wings.

Just seeing them starts my stomach flipping again.

"Time for a last rehearsal," says Zoë. "Skye, you're—"

"I'm not rehearsing," says Mini-Freak.

Zoë's face is hard to read. "Coco, everything's different on stage. I really think you should."

"I don't need to." Coco folds her arms.

"But Coco, the band sounds—"

"I don't want them stealing my moves," says Mini-Freak, nodding at us.

"Excuse me?" says Zoë, hands on her hips.

"Zoë, we clearly have the edge in this

145

competition and want to keep it that way," says Libby. "Coco will not be rehearsing."

Zoë opens and shuts her mouth like a goldfish.

Declan joins us. "You understand we're advising you to practice."

"Yes. And you understand we've made our decision," says Libby.

"Fine," says Declan, his face fierce. "We strongly advise against this, but it's your choice. Wait in the Green Room."

"Thank you," says Libby, guiding Mini-Freak off stage.

Zoë rubs her neck.

Declan shakes his head. "Skye, center stage. Mickey, Mai and Imogen, you can watch from the judges' table."

Chapter Five

Goosebumps pop up along my arms as soon as Skye starts singing. It's like she is the music. Her voice is strong and her dancing so smooth.

"Brilliant, my love," yells Hunter, when she finishes.

"Perfect," says Declan. "Mai's next."

Mai sings *All Star* from *Shrek*. She sounds great at first, but she races the music and loses the beat. She tries to pick it up again, but can't. She bolts from the stage. My heart aches for her.

"Poor thing," says Skye.

"She sucks," says Imogen, skipping to center stage.

"Wow!" I roll my eyes at Skye who raises her eyebrows back at me.

Rocking Robin suits Imogen's little kid voice and curly blonde hair. She's really cute until she gets to the tweeting bit. She does this twinkling thing with her fingers that's seriously weird.

Jed covers his hand with his mouth.

Hunter's eyes widen.

I stare at my beaded shoes.

As Imogen finishes, Mita glides across the stage. "Wonderful, Darling. Perhaps we could change those new hand movements."

"Nah. They're Mom's idea," says Imogen.

My stomach feels weird as I walk across to center stage. I take the microphone from Declan.

The drums start.

Zoë's right. It is different. The sound's fuller and the lights are brighter.

Toes tapping, I count the beat. When I sing my voice is shaky and my dancing jerky. I try to settle down but I can't.

Panic bubbles in my stomach.

Hunter signals "Slow down".

Tight grip on the microphone, I forget about dancing and concentrate on the beat. It works. My voice settles and my dancing improves.

I finish the song without bolting like Mai.

From the wings, Hunter gives me the thumbs up.

"Great song, Mickey," says Declan.

"You were terrific, Mickey," says Skye.

"Not as good as my *Rocking Robin*,' says Imogen, pushing past me.

Skye twinkles her fingertips.

Chapter Six

In the Green Room, a woman dressed in black replaces Mini-Freak's jewelry with bead bracelets and necklaces. Coco looks up and smiles. "This is my stylist, Greta."

"Where's my stylist?" squeals Imogen.

Zoë sighs.

"It's a competition, Zoë." Libby smiles, but her eyes are hard. "Every girl for herself."

"It's against the rules to have a personal stylist, Libby," says Zoë, through clenched teeth .

"Rules?" Mini-Freak's lip curls into a snarl. "If there were real rules, Micala wouldn't be here. Judges' vote? Sympathy vote. She sings like a dying cat and—"

"Enough!" bellows Zoë. "You are way out of line."

Sympathy vote? I slump on the sofa, feeling heavy and tired.

"Libby, Coco, Greta, outside, please," says Zoë.

A lump the size of a tennis ball settles in my throat.

Mom squeezes my knee. "Ignore her, Mickey. She's jealous."

"Of what? My shaky voice? My jerky dancing?"

"That's rubbish, Mickey!" Skye glares at me. "You're here because you're sensational."

"Would you like my herbs?" asks Mai.

"She's fine, thanks," says Mom.

Hunter burst through the stage door. "Righto, breathing exercises, my loves."

I trudge across the room.

"What's up, Mickey?" asks Hunter.

I shrug.

"Coco said Mickey's the sympathy vote and sings like a dying cat." Mai's words run together.

Hunter laughs. "You didn't believe her?"

"I was the judges' choice." My throat hurts and my eyes stings.

"Because Johnny wouldn't know talent if it bit him."

"What about before? I was shaky and—"

"You're too hard on yourself, Mickey." Hunter leans against the keyboard. "I believe in you, but it's what you believe that matters. You can let Coco's jealousy destroy you, or you can go out there and give it your best. What's it going to be?"

"So I can sing?"

Hunter rolls his eyes.

"Absolutely! Now, let's do these breathing exercises."

The lump in my throat shifts and the heavy feeling lifts.

Zoë returns with a hard-faced Libby and Coco, but no Greta.

"Okay guys, to quote two wise girls, Diva is meant to be fun." Zoë winks at Skye and me. "So let's go have fun."

"Hunter, thanks fo—"

"Uh, uh." He hugs me. "Just give it your best."

Mom hugs me next. "Prove her wrong, Mickey," she whispers.

Chapter Seven

Backstage we can hear the warm-up guy firing up the audience.

Jed jogs towards us. "Feeling good?"

"Fantastic," says Coco.

"Sixty seconds," says Declan.

Skye stares at the set. Imogen jogs on the spot, shaking her hands. Mai's face is so white it shines in the backstage gloom.

Coco glares at me and mouths, "Sympathy vote."

No way am I proving her right!

The *Diva TV* theme soars.

"Have a blast," says Jed, high-fiving us and charging onto the set.

The audience roars.

The back of my neck prickles.

"Skye first," says Zoë.

Skye, then Coco, Mai and Imogen step onto the stage.

"Coco's wrong," says Zoë. "You're a fantastic performer."

Warmth floods through me. Grinning, I jog after the others.

The noise, lights and color are dazzling. Excitement bursts through me.

Interview

Jed: *Can you believe Diva's nearly over?*

Skye: *Feels like we only started yesterday.*

Jed: *Mickey, what's been the hardest part of the competition?*

Mickey: *Probably the nerves. My stomach goes crazy before I sing.*

Coco: *Really? I've learned to deal with nerves. Guess it's just experience. I—*

Jed: *Mai, what's been toughest for you?*

Mai: *Being away from home, for sure.*

Skye: *Exactly, being away from home has been tough.*

Jed: *How about you Imogen?*

Imogen: *I hated being near the beach and not being able to swim and surf.*

Coco: *Dealing with difficult people has been tough.*

Jed: *You said it! What's the best thing about Diva?*

Mai: *Everything.*

Mickey: *Yeah everything — singing with Hunter, dancing with Mita. New friends.*

Skye: *Definitely new friends, and singing in front of an audience.*

Imogen: *Shopping and cool clothes. The food's good too!*

Coco: *Being able to share my talent and bring joy to a large audience.*

Jed: *Riiight. Well, we better get down to business. Mickey, like to throw to the break?*

Mickey: *Cool! After the break, the sensational Skye D'Angelo sings on* Diva TV.

Chapter Eight

"Skye, center stage. Coco, backstage. The rest of you, Green Room," yells Declan.

"Good luck," I call to Skye. We're off stage so quickly, I don't get a chance to look for Dad and The Tragics.

In the Green Room, I slip between Mom and Anne on a sofa.

Red nails tapping against her folded arms, Libby paces by the large screen TV.

Suddenly the Diva logo fades and the music starts. Skye sounds even better than at practice.

"She's amazing," says Mom.

"It's like the song was written for her," I whisper.

"Thanks," says her mom, tears in her eyes.

Libby scoffs, "Wait till you hear Coco."

The audience stands and cheers when Skye finishes. Jed strolls across the stage.

"How was that, Skye?"

She grins. "Meg-fun!"

"Fantastic. Let's hear from our first judge, manager of Dream Productions, Gwen Davies."

"Sensational, Skye. You just keep on developing as a performer. I'm giving you 19.5."

"*Misty Beach* and recording star, Sunshine Harris." Jed clicks and points.

"Gwen's right. Wow! Your talent just keeps growing — 19."

"And finally," says Jed, winding up like a baseball pitcher, "TV star extraordinaire, Johnny Mawton."

"Skye, since this competition has

started, you've shown your versatility and skill. You're a talented lass — 18."

I punch the air. Anne cheers.

"Quiet!" yells Libby, now standing in front of the TV.

I have to lean across Mom to see. Mini-Freak has her back to the audience and arms above her head.

"*Material Girl*," I say when the music starts.

"Figures," says Anne.

Mini-Freak shakes her hips and spins. She flutters her eyelids and pouts. She looks strange, but she sounds incredible.

Until she reaches the chorus.

Mini-Freak comes in too early and completely loses her rhythm. She stops singing. The band keeps playing.

Mini-Freak misses one line, then another. It's awful, even for her.

"Want to steal those moves, Imogen?" says Mrs. Beckworth.

"They've sabotaged her," screams Libby, charging out the door.

The camera pans back to show Libby reaching out from behind the set and prodding Mini-Freak in the back. Mini-Freak stumbles, blinks and starts singing.

I breathe out noisily.

"That poor girl," says Mom.

For the rest of the song, Mini-Freak pouts and flutters like crazy. She finishes with a twirl and freezes, arms above her head.

The cheers for Mini-Freak aren't as long or loud as Skye's cheers.

"Coco, great song." Jed pats her back.

Mini-Freak nods, her eyes watery.

"Sunshine, what did you think?"

"Coco, there's no doubt you're a terrific singer, but tonight you seemed under-prepared. Still, you recovered well, and it's your first glitch — 16 points."

Gwen clears her throat.

"What happened, Coco?"

Mini-Freak shrugs.

"Sunshine's right, you are talented, but we haven't seen the same progression in you that we have in others —13."

Johnny slaps the table and glares at Gwen. "What?"

"Coco hasn't developed. Skye, Mickey and Mai keep pushing themselves. Coco's cruising."

Johnny shakes his head. "I can't agree. Coco is a magnificent talent. Tonight was a technical issue — 19 points."

"That makes it 48 for Coco and 56.5 for Skye. Disagree with our judges? Then make sure you vote for your favorite."

Jed winks and pistol points at the camera.

Nineteen? What is it with Johnny and Coco?

"That's ridiculous," says Mrs. Beckworth.

"Mai and Imogen," calls Zoë from the door.

Imogen skips out the door. Mai swigs from her herb bottle and hands it to her mother.

"Have fun," says Skye, breezing into the room.

"You were amazing," says Anne, swallowing Skye in a hug.

"It was ugly backstage." Skye wriggles out of Anne's grip. "I thought Libby was going to punch Zoë."

"It's not Zoë's fault that Mini-Freak wouldn't practice," I say.

"Forget the Lamonts, how did it feel, Skye?" asks Mom.

Skye's face lights up. "Fantastic! You'll love it Mickey!"

When the *Diva TV* theme starts, Mrs. Beckworth turns the TV up so loud the

speakers vibrate. Mrs. Tran stands by the stage door, clutching Mai's bottle.

"Watch Mai with us," yells Mom over the TV.

Mrs. Tran shakes her head. "It's too worrying." She gulps the mixture.

I wish I had herbs to stop my stomach flipping out. Instead I follow Mita's advice and distract myself by concentrating on something else — Mai. It works until Mai mucks up the low notes again.

The rest of her performance is great. She not only makes it through without bolting, but scores 50.

It's easier to be distracted by Imogen, or at least by her mom.

Mrs. Beckworth sings and dances along with Imogen, even twinkling her hands at the same time.

The stage door opens as Jed introduces Johnny, "Mickey," says Zoë.

"Shhhhh!" hisses Mrs. Beckworth

Stomach churning and heart galloping, I walk to the door.

Anne mouths "Good luck."

Skye blows a kiss.

"Have fun, Mickey." Mom kisses me. "Remember, we love you."

My mouth's so dry, I can't speak. I kiss Mom's cheek and slip out the door.

Backstage, I stretch my face, hum scales and think about my dance routine.

Imogen skips off the set. "Fifty-one points. Beat that sucker!" She races to the Green Room.

"Competition brings out the best in some people," says Zoë, frowning.

"You okay?" I ask.

"I'll be better when you've blown everyone away." Smiling, she hands me a microphone.

I step onto the set.

The audience cheers and whistles.

Jed's waiting.

"Have a look around before we start. It'll help."

"Thirty seconds," calls Declan.

"Go for it Mickey!" Jed high-fives me and jogs across the stage.

I smile at the judges. Sunshine blows a kiss. Gwen waves. Johnny nods. At least it's not a frown.

Squinting into the lights, I see Dad and The Tragics in the fourth row. Beside them, waving an enormous "Go Mickey" poster are Hana and Charley.

Suddenly I feel like I can fly.

Declan counts down from ten.

This is it! I wipe my hands on my pants.

"Lucky last finalist, the fantastic Mickey Farrell, singing *Walking on Sunshine*," says Jed, clicking and pointing.

The crowd's cheers are so loud they're scary. Cymbals clash and the drummer beats the introduction.

Icy panic spreads from my tummy to my legs and arms.

Instead of flying, I feel like sprinting — away.

I can't sing and I sure can't dance.

"Sympathy vote" screams my brain.

Just as I'm about to sprint off the stage, I see Dad, The Tragics, Hana and Charley standing and clapping with the beat. A row ahead of them, Erin mouths "Go for it."

I take a deep breath, lift the microphone and sing, right on cue.

My voice is strong and it's like I'm dancing on air. I use the whole stage and even sing to the judges. The audience dances and sings with me.

It's seriously fun! But it's over too quickly.

The audience goes completely nuts.

My whole body buzzes, even my scalp.

Dad wipes his eyes. The Tragics pump the air. Hana and Charley are hugging, clapping and squealing all at once. Erin whistles.

Gwen and Sunshine are on their feet, clapping.

"Mickey, unbelievable," says Jed, beaming. "Was that fun?"

"Seriously fun."

"The audience loved it, but what did Johnny think?"

I clench my fists so tight, my knuckles hurt.

Johnny adjusts his tie. "I'm glad you had fun, Mickey, because I didn't."

The boos and hisses are so loud I block my ears.

"What do you have against this kid?" interrupts Sunshine.

The audience cheers. A chant begins.

"Mickey. Mickey. Mickey."

Johnny raises his hands for quiet.

"In my opinion the performance was pedestrian and erratic — 16."

The jeering is frightening.

"If you disagree, make sure you vote for Mickey yourself." Jed puts his hand on my shoulder. "Gwen, what did you think?"

Gwen stands and claps. "Mickey, you've absolutely wowed us. I've been in this industry a long time, and I know talent. I love you, kid. My first score was 19, but after that fool's comments, it's 20!"

The audience hoot and stamp their feet.

I don't know if it's the pressure, but I laugh.

When the audience settles, Sunshine clears her throat. "Music is about emotions and you've just given us a fun, emotional performance. Top stuff, Mickey — 19 points."

The "Mickey" chant starts again.

My face burns and my skin tingles.

"That's the second-highest score at 55 points. Mickey, is there anything you want to say to Johnny?" asks Jed.

Actually there's a lot I'd like to say, but I don't. "I have heaps to learn, so I appreciate his feedback."

"Good for you Mickey. Let's welcome back the rest of our finalists."

Skye, Mai and Tran gather around Jed and I. Coco rushes to the front of the stage, blowing kisses to the audience.

"Remember, you can vote for your favorite Diva until the start of tomorrow night's show." Jed spins and clicks. "Good night!"

Balloons, streamers and glitter fall from the ceiling. Imogen dances to the *Diva TV* theme. Skye, Mai and I throw balloons and streamers.

Coco stays at the front of the stage.

The lights drop. And it's over.

Chapter Nine

Mom's waiting at the Green Room door. "Mickey, that was terrific."

"You didn't tell me Hana and Charley were coming."

She grins. "Figured you'd like the support."

"Sorry to interrupt." Zoë stands near the TV with Declan, Jed and a guy in a suit. "First of all, congratulations." Zoë looks distracted. "To celebrate, you, your families and the girls from Round Three have Wonderland to yourselves tomorrow."

"Cool!" Imogen bounces on the couch.

"But before we meet your families

at the restaurant, we need to discuss a complaint."

"This competition's a farce!" Libby screeches, flapping into the room with a bearded man and Coco. "My daughter has been unfairly treated."

Mini-Freak sniffs and stares at the floor. The bearded guy with them steps forward. "I'm Mrs. Lamont's lawyer, David Fryer."

"I'm James from the Diva legal team," says the suited guy with Zoë. "Girls, we need your help to work out if there is an issue. Tell me about this evening's final rehearsal."

"You mean on stage?" asks Mai.

"Yes, your last practice with the band," says David.

I take a deep breath. "Mai, Imogen, Skye and I rehearsed with the band. But Coco didn't."

"Why?" asks James.

"Coco said we'd steal her moves," says Imogen in her sing-song voice.

James raises his eyebrows at David. "So she refused to sing?"

"Most definitely," says Mrs. Tran.

"Zoë and Declan tried to convince Coco and Libby." Mom clears her throat. "Look, the issue isn't with the Diva team."

"You would say that. Coco is clearly more gifted than your daughter, and—"

"Stop it." Zoë holds up her hand, palm out, like a policeman stopping traffic. "Libby, your daughter may be talented, but she's a complete pain."

"Mrs. Lamont, I think David will agree, there's no issue," says James.

"It's certainly a different scenario from the one you present, Libby," says David. "It's not an issue."

Libby's face turns purple.

"Settled, then. Let's go meet your families," says Zoë.

Chapter Ten

Balloons bob against the restaurant ceiling and Diva posters hang from the walls. Waiters dressed in Diva T-shirts carry trays of drinks and finger food.

After talking about the show with Mom, Dad and The Tragics, I hang out near the balcony with Charley, Hana, Erin and Skye.

"Wonder where Libby is?" says Skye, nodding at Mini-Freak, her dad and little sister, faces like storm clouds.

"Cooking up trouble," says Erin. "Anyone know where the toilets are?"

"I do," I say.

Erin and I follow the signs past the kitchen and into a courtyard.

Sitting at an outdoor setting are Libby Lamont and Johnny Mawton. I shove Erin into the toilet before they see us.

"What?"

"Shh."

"You promised she'd win," hisses Libby.

"She didn't deserve the score I gave her, Libby."

"And that Mickey Mouse kid did?"

"Libby, Mickey's good — she deserved more than 16."

Erin's eyes are huge. "That rotten cheat!" she whispers.

"You're my cousin." Libby's voice is sharp. "Where's your loyalty?"

I hear seats being pushed across the courtyard brick floor, then heels clicking in our direction.

I dart out the door. "Hi, Mrs. Lamont, Johnny." I smile sweetly.

Erin pops out beside me.

"Beautiful night."

Libby gasps, her eyes wide.

I look up at the inky sky. "Don't voices carry on still nights?"

I'm surprised when Johnny laughs. The color drains from Libby's face.

"See you later," I say, strolling inside with Erin on my heels.

When we tell the others, Skye looks like she'll explode. "You have to tell Zoë."

"Definitely," says Erin.

I shake my head. "What good will it do?"

Chapter Eleven

Dad's puzzling over a map when we arrive at Wonderland.

I tickle him from behind. "Monster Dipper first!"

"How'd you sleep?" He kisses my head.

"Unreal, actually." I'd expected to churn over Johnny and Libby, but I fell asleep straightaway and didn't even dream. "So Monster Dipper?"

Having the park to ourselves is fantastic. No lines and no shoving! The whole day's so much fun, I forget all about tonight.

We meet up with Skye and her family

and Erin and her mom at the Monster Dipper and hang around together for the rest of the day. The Frenetic Frog is my favorite. Erin and Hana keep going back to Mayhem.

Lunch at the restaurant is a yummy barbecue — even better than Dad's. I eat two chicken kebabs and barbecued vegies. Dessert is ice cream and pavlova.

We're leaving the Space Venture ride when the announcement over the park's intercom reminds me why we're here.

"Could Diva Finalists please make their way to the theatre."

My body starts churning, thudding and shaking again.

Dad clears his throat. "Mickey, we're proud of you." He hugs me. "We love you."

There's a heap of hugging before Skye and I make a break for it and run to the theatre.

"What do you think?" asks Kitty, in front of the dressing room mirror.

She's pulled my hair back in this cool, messy style with purple and pink glittery clips that match my dress and shoes.

"Gorgeous," says Mom.

"Thanks heaps, Kitty," I say, trotting out the door.

As soon as I enter the Green Room, Zoë takes us to the stage for a run-through.

Tonight there's no band, just two sofas on the set.

"You walk out together, take a seat and follow Jed's cues, okay?" says Declan.

Sounds simple enough, but Declan has us do it four times before he's happy. Then it's back to the Green Room to wait.

Mai plays cards with her mom, Imogen draws and Coco scowls.

Skye twirls a pink stone. "Rose quartz. Reduces stress," she says when she sees me looking at it.

Wedged in the corner of a sofa, I rub my frog and try the distraction thing. But I keep thinking about tonight's announcement. I'd so love to be the Diva, but honestly, I know Skye's heaps better. Skye winning would be unreal. Just so long as Mini-Freak isn't the Diva.

Mom pats my knee. "Mickey? Are you listening?"

"Moms, you'll watch with your families." Zoë checks her watch. "It's time to go."

The icy feeling in my stomach spreads to my chest and thighs. Mom kisses me. "Mickey, I'm so proud I could burst. No competition can change that."

I throw my arms around her, then bolt for the door.

The judges, Jed and Declan are waiting backstage.

"Girls, you've been a pleasure to work with," says Gwen.

"This is just the beginning for all of you," says Sunshine,

"Exactly," says Johnny.

Suddenly everyone's hugging and patting each other on the back.

Johnny leans in towards me. "When you first sang, I knew you were the biggest threat to Coco. I have probably been harder on you than the other girls. For that I apologize, Mickey." He shakes my hand. "Good luck."

All I can think is "Wow."

Declan counts down and the Diva theme plays.

Jed jogs onto the set.

The audience roars.

Jed introduces the judges and runs through the whole Diva process.

Backstage, Mai sucks on her herbs, Imogen bounces on her toes and Skye slips her crystal into her skirt pocket. I rub my frog and try to control my breathing.

Mini-Freak stands apart from us, rolling her shoulders.

"Think she's nervous?" I ask Mai.

"No way," says Mai. "She's so sure she's won, she's written a speech."

"Maybe we should have told Zoë about, you know, the whole Cousin Johnny thing," says Skye, chewing her bottom lip.

But it's too late for that now.

"Please welcome our five amazing finalists," says Jed.

Mini-Freak charges onto the stage, followed by Imogen and Mai.

"Good luck," says Zoë, patting Skye and me on the back.

The lights and noise are dazzling.

Waving, Skye and I walk to the couches. Our families sit together in the fourth row, again. Erin sits in the row in front with all the other girls from Round Three, except Liberty Wilde.

Skye elbows me. "Look."

Mini-Freak's down in the audience, high-fiving the people in the front row. When she finally joins us, she pushes Mai aside to sit closest to Jed.

"So Divas, how are you?" asks Jed.

"Fine." Mini-Freak smooths her skirt and smiles.

"Scared," says Imogen, bouncing on the couch.

"Bit sad, actually," I say.

"How come, Mickey?"

"I'll miss everyone." Well, not quite everyone, but I can't say everyone except Mini-Freak. "It's been the best fun."

"Sure has. Let's take a look at the Diva journey," says Jed.

The *Diva TV* logo fills the monitor screen and boppy music signals the beginning of a film clip. There's Erin pulling a face, Coco strutting across the stage, Imogen handstanding across

the stage, and all of us shopping with Nar-Tar-Shar. The last shot is of me and Skye eating dinner in our pajamas.

My throat's tight and my eyes sting. It's weird; all at once I'm happy and sad.

"It's been a blast, guys, but now the Diva journey has to end." Jed pulls a sad face. "After the break, the decision."

"Clear!" Declan, jumps on stage, hands Jed an envelope and walks him to center stage.

Rubbing my frog, I wave to Mom and Dad. Declan counts Jed in and scuttles off-stage. I take a deep breath. Dad blows me a kiss. Erin waves her crossed fingers.

Someone signals we're back on and the audience applauds.

"Judges, before we announce the winner, who do you think will win?" asks Jed.

Gwen sighs. "All five girls have been sensational, but I think it's between

Mickey and Skye."

My face burns. No way. Skye for sure.

"I can't choose one," says Sunshine, screwing up her face.

I suck in my breath, ready for Johnny's Mini-Freak rave.

Johnny smooths his tie. "The immense pressure I've been under during this competition has clouded my judgement." He looks from Mini-Freak to me. "I trust the voters have seen what I missed and have voted on talent and personality."

"Wow," says Jed, nodding. "Thanks Johnny. Well, let's not draw this out." He pulls the envelope from his pocket.

Mini-Freak pulls a slip of paper from her waistband and sits forward.

Mai closes her eyes.

Imogen, kicking the sofa, chews her thumb. Skye twirls her crystal. I grab her other hand. She squeezes so hard it hurts.

Jed opens the envelope and smiles. "It's been a tight contest between two girls, but we do have a winner."

Mini-Freak, paper unfolded, stands.

"Our Diva is..."

The drum roll is deafening.

"...Skye D'Angelo."

The audience jumps to its feet and roars.

Tears fill Skye's eyes. "Seriously?"

"This is perfect," I say, hugging her.

We're swamped by Gwen, Sunshine, Johnny, Mai and Imogen.

Mini-Freak looks as though she's been punched in the stomach.

Jed leads Skye to center stage.

"Skye D'Angelo, our Diva."

He waits for the whistles and cheers to stop. "Skye, you've won a recording contract, personal tuition with choreographer Mita and voice-coach Hunter, plus heaps of cool stuff like computers, CDs and clothes. How does it feel?"

"Sensational," squeaks Skye.

"But there's more."

Skye grabs her stomach. "Now what?"

Jed laughs. "*Girls Stuff TV* starts next week, and,' Jed whips himself into a clicking and pointing storm, "you, our Diva, are the host."

"You're kidding!" Skye squeals and spins around to face me. "Do you believe this?"

Arms folded and legs crossed, Mini-Freak scowls.

"But," Jed goes all serious. "There's a catch."

Skye groans softly. "Not another competition."

"We'll find out — right after this break." Jed winks.

During the commercial, Kitty fusses over Skye until Declan chases her off the

stage. I watch, feeling seriously happy for Skye, and just the tiniest bit jealous.

"So Skye... Diva," says Jed, when the show returns. "The catch..." He winks and points, "...is, we need a co-host."

Mini-Freak unfolds her arms and smiles.

"Can I pick?" says Skye, hands clasped in front of her heart.

"Actually, the other girls from Round Two and the judges voted during the break."

Erin leads the 20 girls voted off in Round Two onto the set and behind the sofas. She jumps into Skye's empty seat next to me.

"Nervous?" she asks.

"Not really. Mai's so sweet, she'll win."

"She wasn't my vote," says Erin.

Jed spins and pistol points to the judges. "Johnny, who is Skye's co-host?"

Johnny clears his throat and smiles.

I groan. Any hope I had of winning disappears. Johnny's never smiled for me.

"Mini-Freak's about to get a TV career," I whisper to Erin.

"I'm thrilled to announce…"

Mini-Freak flicks her hair and, nose in the air, walks to center stage.

"…the co-host for *Girls Stuff TV* is…"

I lean and whisper to Erin. "Poor Skye." Only Erin's not there. She's jumping and screaming in front of me.

Skye's with her now. They grab my hands and pull me to my feet.

"What's going on?" I yell.

"You're it!' screams Skye. "You're hosting *Girls Stuff TV* with me."

"What?"

Sunshine slips between Erin and Skye. "Fantastic. I'm so thrilled."

Still confused I look around.

Mini-Freak, mouth hanging open and speech still in her hand, looks from me

to Johnny like she can't believe what's happening.

"There's been a mistake!" she says, her eyes becoming hard.

But no one's listening.

Mom's grinning and crying. Dad, The Tragics, Hana and Charley are hooting and clapping.

"What do you mean?"

Sunshine grins and leads Skye and me to Gwen, Johnny and Jed, center stage.

"Skye, are you happy with your co-host?" asks Jed.

"Happy? If I had a choice it would definitely be Mickey!"

"Congratulations, Mickey. How do you feel about working with Skye?" asks Jed, his smile so big, he might burst.

I might just burst, too.

Everything — missing my family, the fight with Erin, not being able to hang out with Hana and Charley at school,

Mini-Freak's nastiness and my shoe disaster — everything has been worth it.

I feel Coco's eyes burning into me, like a laser beam on full power. But even she can't spoil this moment.

"I feel amazing!" I jump into the air. "Bring on *Girls Stuff TV*!"

Glossary

Audition — To try out for a role or position.

Backstage — Rear of the stage which is out of the sight of the audience.

Center stage — Middle of the stage.

Choreographer — Person who creates dance routines.

Dress rehearsal — A full rehearsal, with all the costumes, music and lighting.

Dressing rooms — Rooms where performers change into costumes.

Floor manager — Person who works on the studio floor, telling the cast and crew what to do.

Green Room — Room where performers rest when not onstage. They aren't always green.

Make-up artist — Applies make-up to performers. TV performers wear special make-up because the lights make them look pale and blotchy.

Monitors — Special TV sets placed around the set so performers can see the program.

Pan — To move a movie or television camera to follow an object or create a panoramic effect.

Offstage — Any position near the stage out of sight of the audience.

Onstage — Any position on the stage within the acting area.

Set — Background scenery.

Studio lights — Bright lights used in TV studios.

Wings — The sides of the stage, out of sight of the audience. Performers wait in the wings before going on stage.

Quiz One

Are you a stress nut or a cool cucumber?

1. **You're asked to do a talk for your class. Do you...**

A. Spend the whole week writing and rewriting pages of information?

B. Write a few points down the night before?

C. Work out what you'll say the morning of your talk?

2. **You see your fave actor shopping in the city. Do you...**

A. Follow, at a very big distance and hope he doesn't notice?

B. Rush up and ask him for his autograph?

C. Rush up and ask him to join you and your mom for lunch?

3. **Your teacher asks you to stay back after school. Do you...**

A. Freak out, wondering what you've done wrong?

B. Wonder for a moment if you're in trouble, but not think about it again till after school?

C. Decide she's so impressed with your work she wants to offer you a scholarship?

4. **Your mom has an early start. She leaves a list of jobs for you on the kitchen table. Do you...**

A. Do the jobs straightaway, and then worry all day that you might have forgotten one?

B. Decide to do them as soon as you get home from school and forget about it till then?

C. Remember the note as your mom pulls up in the driveway and still manage to do everything on her list?

5. Your school is putting on a musical production. Do you...

A. Try out for an offstage position, like the lighting?

B. Go for a role in the chorus or as an extra?

C. Try out for the lead role?

6. You decide to organize a surprise party for your best bud. Do you...

A. Try to organize everything on your own and end up freaking out?

B. Gather a group of buds and share the load?

C. Not even remember it's your best friend's birthday?

Quiz Two

Pushover or Plain Pushy?
What type of friend are you?

1. What type of animal would you like to be?
A. Labrador dog?
B. Persian cat?
C. Dwarf rabbit?

2. All of your friends forget your birthday. Are you...
A. A bit upset, because you never forget their birthdays?
B. Furious? How could they forget your birthday?
C. Okay about it, it's only your birthday?

3. What type of things do you like to do with your friends?
A. Whatever you all choose that's fun.
B. Talk about you and your problems.
C. Anything they want to do.

4. What's the best thing about having friends?

A. Having fun and being there for each other.

B. Having people to do stuff you want to do with.

C. Having someone let you hang around with them.

5. You friend tells you an amazing piece of gossip and swears you to secrecy. Do you?

A. Tell no one, not even your teddy?

B. Broadcast it. What's gossip if you can't be the one to spread it?

C. Tell one other friend and swear them to secrecy?

6. Two of your best friends have a huge fight. Do you...

A. Get them together and try to help them sort it out?

B. De-friend one or both? Who needs the hassle?

C. Listen to both sides but not take a side?

7. **Your best friend has a mega-crush on a really geeky guy. She asks you what you think of him. Do you...**

A. Say you really don't know him well enough to say what you think?

B. Tell her how geeky he is, loud and often?

C. Tell her you think he's mega-cool?

8. **Your school's putting on a musical and you and your best friend want the lead role. Do you...**

A. Talk about it and decide no matter what, you'll stay friends?

B. Stop talking to her and tell everyone she's temperamental and hard to work with?

C. Not audition so she'll get the part for sure?

Answers
Quiz One

Mostly A...

Boy, are you a Stress Nut! Time you took up Tai Chi or meditation. Relax — it's never as bad as you think! Kick back and have a little fun!

Mostly B...

You're a pretty cool customer! You do what you can to make sure things go smoothly and aren't afraid to live on the edge, just a little.

Mostly C...

Does anything worry you? You're a little too calm, even in the face of major danger, like a furious parent. A little stress could do you good!

Answers
Quiz Two

Mostly A...

What an awesome friend! You're loyal and treat other people with respect. Make sure you have fun too and don't take life too seriously.

Mostly B...

Wow, ease up girl. It's okay to put yourself first, but not all the time. Think about other people's feelings and listen to their opinions.

Mostly C...

You're a kind-hearted, giving person, but you put everyone else first. Be careful people don't push you around and take you for granted. It's okay to think of yourself first.